THE SHERIFF'S CHRISTMAS ANGEL

GRACE SPRINGFIELD

ISBN 978-1-918219-53-1

First Edition: 2025
Published by: Cosmic Jive Publishing

www.cosmicjivepublishing.com

For permissions and inquiries, contact:
info@cosmicjivepublishing.com

Disclaimer:

This is a work of fiction. Names, characters, businesses, places, events, locales, and incidents are either the products of the author's imagination or used in a fictitious manner. Any resemblance to actual persons, living or dead, or actual events is purely coincidental.

CHAPTER 1

Ellie Freeman had always believed that December in Colorado was God's way of showing off—a sweep of frosted pines and diamond-dusted air, where every breath felt sharper and cleaner, like the world itself was paying attention.

She no longer believed in much of anything else—and that loss felt heavier than the snow. Once, she'd been certain places like Estrella Ridge were the problem—too small, too narrow, too content with surface smiles and recycled traditions. Twelve years ago, she'd fled for cities that promised depth and meaning, convinced significance only existed where streets were louder and ambitions sharper. Funny how those places had taught her the opposite: how easy it was to be surrounded by millions and still live a life skimming the surface.

The windshield wipers fought a losing battle against the snow as her SUV crawled along the winding mountain road, each turn revealing another postcard-perfect vista that she was too numb to appreciate. The radio had given up twenty miles back, leaving only the rhythmic thump of tires on packed ice and the low hum of a worship song she'd turned down so quietly she could pretend she wasn't listening. The familiar melody—one she'd sung in church every Christmas Eve growing up—felt like both a comfort and an accusation.

O come, O come, Emmanuel, and ransom captive Israel...

She used to think towns like Estrella Ridge survived on nostalgia and nothing else—borrowed meaning, passed down like heirlooms no one questioned. Back then, she'd believed cities were where depth lived, where ideas mattered and lives weren't reduced to who your parents were or what church you attended.

Funny how the city had taught her how easy it was to disappear. How loneliness could hide in crowds. How shallowness didn't belong to places at all—but to people afraid to be known.

Thirty-one years old, divorced (or as good as), and pregnant by a man who despite being married to her hadn't wanted either permanence or responsibility—Ellie Freeman had the uncomfortable sense that irony was God's favorite language.

She was three miles from Estrella Ridge—three miles from the house she'd sworn she would never set foot in again—when the road decided it had had enough of her.

It happened faster than she could process. One moment she was gripping the steering wheel with white-knuckled determination, eyes fixed on the faint tire tracks ahead. The next, the back end of the SUV slid first in what felt like slow motion, a graceful betrayal that made her stomach drop. Ellie corrected too hard, overcorrecting the way her driver's ed teacher had warned her against fifteen years ago. She felt the tires lose their last whisper of traction, and then the world tilted sideways in a way that defied all logic.

Pines rushed up to meet her windshield like they'd been waiting for this moment. The seat belt snapped tight across her chest, cutting into her collarbone with bruising force. The last thing she saw before the airbag exploded was the ridiculous plastic nativity scene still suction-cupped to her dashboard—a leftover from the moving truck she'd driven out of Nevada this morning, something she'd meant to throw away but hadn't quite been able to.

The baby Jesus in that cheap plastic manger seemed to stare at her with knowing eyes—like He'd seen this coming.

Then everything went white and mercifully quiet.

The world stopped spinning eventually, though it took Ellie several long moments to realize it. Her ears rang with a high-pitched whine that drowned out everything else. The engine was dead, the sudden silence almost as shocking as the crash itself. The air smelled like burnt rubber and pine needles and something chemical from the deployed airbag. Her heart was trying to hammer its way out of her ribs, each beat so hard she could feel it in her throat.

Ellie sat very still, taking inventory the way her father had taught her when she was eight and learning to drive the ranch truck around the property: fingers—she wiggled them one by one—ten, all present and accounted for. Legs—she flexed her ankles carefully—two, both responding. Baby—she pressed one trembling hand low on her belly, just beginning to curve beneath her loose sweater—still there, thank You, God, or maybe just thank you, luck, or fate, or whatever force in the universe was still looking out for fools who drove mountain roads in snowstorms.

She couldn't quite bring herself to pray the way she used to. The words still existed somewhere inside her—they just didn't line up neatly anymore. The words felt rusty, unused, like a door that had been locked so long the hinges had seized.

Snow hissed against the cracked windshield, an angry whisper that promised the storm was far from over. The road was gone, replaced by a steep embankment and a stand of evergreens that had, mercifully, broken her fall. Through the driver's side window, she could see where her SUV had carved a path through virgin snow, leaving a scar of churned earth and broken branches.

She reached for her phone with fingers that wouldn't quite cooperate, fumbling in the cup holder where she'd left it. The screen was spider-webbed with cracks—when had that happened?—but it still lit up when she pressed the home button. No signal. Of course. She was in a dead zone, had been since she'd left the main highway fifteen miles back.

Ellie laughed once, a short, sharp sound that came out a little hysterical, then pressed both gloved hands to her mouth until the sound died in her throat. Hysteria wouldn't help. Panic wouldn't help. She needed to think, needed to act, needed to do something other than sit here while the temperature dropped and the snow piled higher.

Get out. Get warm. Get help.

The words became a mantra as she fumbled with her

seatbelt, fingers clumsy in her thick gloves. It took three tries before the buckle released with a click that sounded impossibly loud. She shoved the door open against the drift of snow that had already begun to pile against the SUV, using her shoulder when it stuck halfway.

The cold hit like a physical slap, stealing her breath and making her eyes water instantly. She'd thought it was cold inside the car, but that was nothing compared to this. The wind cut through her wool coat like it wasn't even there, finding every gap and seam. She stepped out into snow that swallowed her boots to mid-shin, and immediately her feet went numb.

Ellie was tugging her scarf higher, trying to cover her nose and mouth against the biting wind, when red and blue lights flickered through the trees. Faint at first, easy to mistake for a trick of the snow and her rattled brain. Then stronger, cutting through the storm like a promise, like an answer to a prayer she hadn't quite let herself pray.

A sheriff's SUV eased to a stop twenty yards up the road where the pavement was still visible, hazard lights blinking in steady rhythm. He must have been running weather patrol—checking the mountain roads before the storm trapped someone overnight.

The driver's door opened and a man unfolded himself from the cab—tall, broad-shouldered, the kind of tall that made the Stetson on his head look almost reasonable instead of ridiculous. He moved like someone used to storms, boots crunching with purpose as he made his way toward her, one hand on his hat to keep the wind from stealing it.

"Ma'am? You all right?"

The voice was low, calm, pure Colorado baritone with the faintest hint of gravel. The kind of voice that probably worked wonders on panicked citizens—and spooked horses—alike. Ellie shaded her eyes against the snow and the glare of headlights. When he got close enough for the floodlight mounted on his cruiser to catch his face, something inside her chest did a traitorous little flip that had nothing to do with the accident.

Caleb Brennan—of course it was.

Of course it was Caleb Brennan. Because the universe had apparently decided that one humiliation per hour wasn't enough, that she needed to face the boy—no, the man now—she'd been half in love with in high school while covered in airbag dust and possibly about to burst into tears.

He didn't recognize her yet. The brim of his hat shadowed his eyes, and twelve years of city life plus a metric ton of emotional baggage had changed her more than she liked to admit. Her hair was longer now, lighter from spending more time in the sun. She wore different makeup, different clothes, carried herself differently. She was different, right down to her bones.

She opened her mouth to answer his question and discovered her teeth were chattering too hard to form words. The adrenaline was wearing off, leaving behind bone-deep cold and exhaustion.

Caleb took in the SUV nose-first in the ditch, then her, then the small duffel bag she'd managed to drag out of the back seat before her hands got too cold to grip anything. His jaw tightened almost imperceptibly.

"Anyone else in the vehicle?" His tone was professional, efficient, the kind he'd probably use with any stranded motorist.

She shook her head, not trusting her voice yet.

"Good." He was already moving, turning back toward his cruiser with long strides. "Let's get you warm first, then we'll figure out the rest."

He returned moments later with a thick wool blanket, the kind that emergency responders kept in their vehicles for exactly this kind of situation. The blanket smelled like woodsmoke and something that might have been pine soap, clean and masculine and unexpectedly comforting. He wrapped it around her shoulders himself, big hands gentle but impersonal, the way you'd handle a skittish colt that might bolt at any moment.

"This'll help until we get you to the—" He stopped mid-sentence as he stepped back and tipped his hat higher to really look at her face.

The recognition hit him like a rifle's recoil. She saw it in the slight widening of storm-gray eyes, in the way his mouth went flat, in the minute pause before he spoke again.

"Ellie Freeman." It wasn't a question, just a statement of fact delivered in a carefully neutral tone.

"Hello, Caleb." She tried for a smile; it felt more like a grimace, her frozen facial muscles not quite cooperating. "Still pulling foolish females out of snowbanks, I see."

Something flickered across his face—surprise, maybe, or memory, or some complicated combination of both—then settled back into professional sheriff-neutral. But his eyes lingered on her face a moment longer than strictly necessary, like he was trying to reconcile the girl he'd known with the woman standing in front of him.

"Looks like some things don't change." He glanced at the wrecked SUV again, assessing the damage with a practiced eye. "You hurt? Any pain, dizziness, blurred vision?"

"No. Just my pride." She pulled the blanket tighter around herself, grateful for its warmth. "And maybe my car insurance premiums."

"SUV took the worst of it. Those trees probably saved you from something a lot worse." He looked back up the embankment toward the road, calculating angles and distances. "You're lucky. Another few yards and—"

He didn't finish the sentence, but he didn't need to. They both knew what he meant.

A small voice piped up from inside the cruiser, high and clear despite the wind. "Daddy, is the lady okay?"

Ellie hadn't noticed the child in the passenger seat—a boy bundled in a puffy coat that looked two sizes too big, round cheeks red from the heater, eyes the exact color of his father's fixed on her with the unself-conscious intensity that only children possessed. He had a candy cane clutched in one small fist and a look of pure eight-year-old fascination on his face, like watching his dad rescue stranded motorists was the most exciting thing that had happened all week.

The word *Daddy* landed like a quiet blow.

Of course.

Marriage, a child, a whole life she'd missed. She swallowed the sharp edge of disappointment that had no right to exist after twelve years and a thousand miles. She'd left this town because she'd wanted more—more than Friday night football, more than a future everyone else had already planned for her, more than a life that felt decided before it even began. She'd wanted momentum, meaning, proof she wasn't meant to stay small.

Apparently, Caleb Brennan hadn't needed to leave to find those things.

"She's fine, Noah," Caleb said without turning, his voice gentling automatically when he addressed his son. "Stay put, bud. Keep the heater running."

Noah considered this for approximately three seconds, clearly weighing the merits of obedience against his burning curiosity. Curiosity won. The door cracked open and a small blizzard of snow blew into the warm interior, making Caleb's jaw tighten again.

"Hi, lady!" Noah called out, waving his candy cane like a beacon. "I'm Noah. Are you gonna die?" he asked, curious rather than afraid.

"Noah James." Caleb's tone could have frozen the snow midair, a perfect balance of parental exasperation and warning.

Ellie laughed despite everything—the cold, the shock, the surreal situation. It came out wobbly but real, surprising her with its genuine warmth. Something about the boy's earnest concern and complete lack of filter cut through her carefully maintained composure.

"I'm not planning on it, Noah. I'm Ellie." She took a tentative step toward the cruiser, her legs steadier now.

Noah's grin was missing two front teeth, giving him a jack-o'-lantern quality that was utterly endearing. "Daddy, she's pretty. Can we keep her?" he asked, as if this were a perfectly reasonable request.

Heat flooded Ellie's face despite the frigid temperature—and beneath the embarrassment, something else stirred. If Noah talked like that, if his mother wasn't here… then Caleb wasn't married. Divorced, likely as not. Like she was about to be.

The realization settled cautiously, unwelcome and dangerous and far too hopeful for someone who had sworn she was done wanting things that complicated.

Caleb closed his eyes for one long-suffering second that spoke volumes about life with an precocious eight-year-old, then opened them with the air of a man who had learned to pick his battles.

He opened the back door of his cruiser with a gesture that brooked no argument. "Inside, both of you. Now."

It didn't surprise her as sheriff's kid was riding along. Storm nights meant school closures and no babysitters willing to drive mountain roads. Ellie remembered that part of small-town life— parents improvising, kids riding along, everyone doing what they had to.

Ellie started to protest—she had a perfectly good duffel bag, she could walk to town, she didn't need to impose on him more than she already had—but the wind chose that precise moment to knife straight through her coat with vindictive precision. Her body made the decision before her pride could object, every muscle trembling with cold and delayed shock.

Caleb's hand settled at the small of her back, warm even through the layers of blanket and coat, guiding her forward with the quiet authority of a man who had decided arguing was pointless. His touch was steady, impersonal, but somehow reassuring in a way she hadn't expected.

She slid into the warm interior that smelled faintly of coffee, fast food, and little-boy sneakers. The heat from the vents felt like heaven against her frozen skin. Noah scooted over to make room without being asked, immediately offering her half of his candy cane like it was a peace treaty, a sacred offering.

"It's peppermint," he informed her solemnly. "The red part

tastes more minty than the white part. I did experiments."

"Thank you." Ellie accepted it with equal gravity, wrapping her numb fingers around the sticky offering. "That's very scientific of you."

Noah beamed at the praise, settling back into his seat with the satisfied air of a diplomat who had successfully brokered peace.

She'd barely settled into the seat when something warm and solid pressed against her leg. A dog's enthusiastic snort followed, then a tail thumped hard against the door panel like it had been waiting for permission all along.

'Tripod," Noah explained.

"Cool name!' Ellie smiled.

She was about to ask why when Tripod shifted, planting his weight enthusiastically against her leg, tail thumping like a drumbeat. Any coherent question vanished as he shoved his head into her lap, clearly convinced she existed solely for petting purposes.

Caleb climbed behind the wheel, bringing with him a gust of cold air and snowflakes that melted immediately in the warmth. He put the SUV in gear with careful precision, checking his mirrors out of habit even though they were the only vehicle on this stretch of road. Then he glanced at Ellie in the rearview mirror, and she saw something flicker in his eyes before he shuttered it away.

"House on Sparrow Lane still standing?" His voice was carefully neutral, but there was a question underneath the question.

Of course he knew which house. Everyone in town knew which house—knew about Grandma Ruth, about the scandal, about why Ellie had left and never come back. Small towns had long memories and persistent gossip mills.

"For now," she said, her own voice matching his neutral tone.

He nodded once, accepting this, and pulled onto the road with the kind of careful control that suggested he'd driven through worse storms than this. "Then that's where we're headed."

The wipers beat a steady rhythm against the windshield, fighting a battle they couldn't quite win. Snow blurred the world beyond the windows into watercolor whites and grays, turning familiar landmarks into ghostly suggestions. Ellie clutched the blanket tighter around herself and tried not to notice how Noah had inched closer until his small shoulder pressed against hers, seeking contact with the unconscious ease of a child who'd been taught that people were generally safe and kind.

Caleb's eyes in the mirror kept finding hers and then flicking away, like he was checking to make sure she was real—like this was actually happening.

Welcome home, she thought with bitter irony. *Merry stinking Christmas.*

She rested one gloved hand low on her belly where no one could see, where the secret she carried was still safe, still hers alone. The baby—barely more than a flutter, a whisper of movement—seemed to turn over inside her, as if responding to her thoughts.

We're going to be okay, she told the tiny life inside her silently. *We have to be.*

She prayed the roads were the worst thing this town had in store for her, even though deep down, she already knew better.

She should have known that coming home never meant just facing old houses and frozen pipes. It meant facing everything she'd left behind—including the boy who'd grown into a man who could still make her heart skip with just a glance in a rearview mirror.

The SUV's tires hummed against the packed snow, carrying them all toward whatever came next.

Chapter 2

The heater in Caleb's cruiser roared like an angry bear, but it still took three blocks before Ellie's fingers stopped tingling with that painful transition from numb to feeling. Estrella Ridge rolled past the windows in slow motion, each familiar landmark hitting her with unexpected force.

There was Morrison's Hardware, its brick facade now painted a cheerful red instead of the faded brown she remembered. The store window displayed artificial Christmas trees and strings of lights arranged in elaborate patterns. Henderson's Diner still occupied the corner of Main and Third, its neon sign flickering the same way it had when she was sixteen and nursing Cherry Cokes while pretending to study for chemistry tests.

The same candy-cane lampposts lined the streets—the ones she used to bike past on summer evenings when the world felt infinite and full of possibility. The same storefronts, though some had different names now. The same everything, and yet somehow different. Like looking at a photograph that had faded slightly, colors not quite as bright as memory insisted they should be.

Only the Christmas lights looked brighter than she remembered, as if the town had decided to overcompensate for something. Every storefront, every lamppost, every tree on the square blazed with illumination. Garland wrapped around telephone poles. Wreaths hung on every door. It was aggressively festive, determinedly cheerful, the kind of small-town Christmas that belonged on a Hallmark card.

It made Ellie's throat tight for reasons she didn't want to examine.

A thump came from behind her seat, followed by impatient snuffling—something large and determined making its presence known long before formal introductions.

Noah twisted around in the front seat to stare at her openly, his candy cane now reduced to a stub of sticky sweetness. "Do you like dogs?"

Ellie blinked at the sudden question, her tired brain taking a moment to process the question. "I—what?"

"'Cause Tripod likes you." Noah pointed toward the cargo area behind Ellie's seat with the confidence of someone stating an obvious fact. "Tripod likes everybody," Noah added seriously, as if clarifying an important scientific principle. "But he likes you extra."

A wet nose shoved itself between the seats, followed by a brindle head the size of a basketball. The dog was some kind of mixed breed—maybe pit bull, maybe boxer, definitely something with enthusiasm genes. One ear stood straight up in permanent alert; the other flopped over like it had given up trying. His tongue lolled out in a doggy grin that radiated pure joy.

But it was the back leg—or rather, the missing back leg—that made Ellie's heart squeeze. The evident reason for his name, she realized. The dog was missing most of his left rear leg, the fur at the shoulder growing over the old scar tissue. But he didn't seem to notice or care. He planted his single hind foot on the console with surprising stability, tail whipping hard enough to rattle the handcuffs hanging from the dash, and licked Ellie's cheek with enthusiastic devotion.

"Tripod!" Caleb reached across with one hand, trying to corral the dog while keeping his eyes on the snowy road. "Down. I swear he's never this bad with strangers."

"He's perfect," Ellie heard herself say, and meant it. Something about the dog's crooked grin and absolute confidence in his own magnificence loosened the knot in her chest that had been there since Nevada, since the divorce papers–the divorce she'd sworn she'd never let happen but it was happening to her anyway–since the morning she'd taken the pregnancy test and watched her entire future rearrange itself.

She scratched behind the good ear, finding the spot that made Tripod's back foot kick reflexively. He groaned in bliss and collapsed across her lap like a fifty-pound heating pad, apparently deciding this human was acceptable.

Noah beamed with proprietary pride. "See, Daddy? He picked her. That means she's supposed to stay."

Caleb's eyes flicked to the rearview mirror again, lingered a half-second too long, then returned to the road. His jaw worked like he was choosing his words carefully. "We got Tripod from a shelter. Keeps escaping. Force of habit, I guess. Third time this month I've had to collect him from somewhere he shouldn't be."

"It was just as well he did, this time, Dad, or we would not have seen the lady!"

Noah grunted an acknowledgment, a smile tugging at the corner of his mouth. His eyes were inscrutable.

They turned onto Sparrow Lane, and Ellie's breath caught despite herself. The street looked like something from a Christmas movie—pristine snow covering perfect lawns, lights twinkling from every eave, wreaths on every door. And at the end of the cul-de-sac, rising like a tired queen surveying her domain, stood Grandma Ruth's house.

The Victorian was exactly as she remembered and somehow worse. Three stories of gingerbread trim, once painted in cheerful blues and whites, now faded to gray and cream. The wraparound porch sagged slightly on the east side, the way it had been threatening to do for years. Every window was dark except the attic gable where a single bulb glowed—Grandma Ruth's old "I'm-still-alive" signal to the neighbors, though Ruth had been gone six months now.

Someone was still paying the electric bill. Probably the estate lawyer, keeping the utilities on until everything was settled. Snow had piled on the steps in perfect, untouched drifts—beautiful and melancholy.

Caleb killed the engine but made no move to get out immediately. For a long moment no one spoke. The silence felt thick, full of things neither adult wanted to say in front of an eight-year-old with excellent hearing and, Ellie had already worked out, a tendency to repeat everything at inappropriate moments.

Noah, blessedly, broke the tension first. "Can she come in with us? Just till the storm stops? It's almost suppertime and Mrs. Mabel says strangers shouldn't be alone at Christmas. She says it's in the Bible."

"I'm hardly a stranger," Ellie said softly, though she wasn't sure if that was true anymore. Twelve years was a long time. Long enough to become a stranger to a place that had once been home.

Caleb exhaled through his nose, a long breath that fogged in the rapidly cooling interior. "Noah, go let Tripod out back. Give us a minute."

Noah opened his mouth to argue—she could see the protest forming—but caught his father's look and thought better of it. He unbuckled with exaggerated care, clipped a leash to Tripod's collar with the practiced ease of someone who'd done this a thousand times, and the two of them tumbled out into the snow like conspirators on a secret mission.

The doors shut. Quiet descended again, heavier this time.

Caleb turned in his seat so he could see her straight on, one arm draped across the steering wheel. Snowflakes melted on the brim of his hat, leaving dark spots on the felt. In the dim light, his face was all angles and shadows, but his eyes were kind. They'd always been kind, she remembered. Even when he'd been a teenage boy trying to seem tough, his eyes had given him away.

"You okay to walk, or you want me to carry you to the porch?" His voice was matter-of-fact, no judgment in it.

"I can walk." She hugged the blanket tighter around herself, suddenly aware that accepting his help felt like crossing some invisible line. "I'm not an invalid."

"Didn't say you were." A pause, weighted with things unsaid. "You sure you're not hurt? No pain anywhere? Accident like that, sometimes the adrenaline hides things."

"I'm fine." The lie tasted metallic on her tongue. She wasn't fine—she was bruised, shaken, three months pregnant by a man who'd told her children would ruin her figure and destroy her career, and was currently homeless in the town she'd sworn never to return to. But fine was easier than the truth.

Caleb studied her the way he probably studied crime scenes —quiet, thorough, missing nothing. She had the uncomfortable sensation of being read like a book with large print.

"Ruth's house has been empty six months," he said finally. "Furnace is probably frozen. Pipes too. Town plumber told me last week he wouldn't even look at that place until spring. You can't stay there tonight. Probably not for a few days, honestly. And in this cold? Frozen pipes turn into flooded houses fast."

"I have a hotel reservation in Durango—" she started, but he was already shaking his head.

"Road's closed over the pass till morning at least. Storm's sitting on us like a broody hen, and the forecast says it's not moving till tomorrow afternoon." He rubbed the back of his neck, a gesture she vaguely remembered from high school when he was working through a difficult problem. "I've got a spare room. Noah will be thrilled. You can argue if you want, but you won't win."

Ellie opened her mouth, then closed it. The idea of sleeping in her grandmother's cold, empty house—surrounded by thirty years of memories and the faint smell of lilac water that would still be clinging to the curtains—made her throat close up. The idea of accepting charity from Caleb Brennan, of all people, wasn't much better. But what choice did she have?

"I'm not the girl you knew in high school, Caleb." The words came out sharper than she intended.

"Didn't figure you were." His voice remained gentle, patient. "But it's a bed, it's warm, and Noah's already planning pancakes shaped like reindeer for breakfast. One night. Tomorrow we'll get your car towed and figure the rest out. No strings, no expectations. Just a warm place to sleep and breakfast with an eight-year-old who asks approximately six hundred questions per hour."

She looked at the house again, at the dark windows that

seemed to stare back at her accusingly. The porch swing creaked in the wind, moving in slow arcs despite the snow weighing down its chains. Empty. Waiting. Judging.

Grandma Ruth would have marched straight through the snow, opened her door to anyone who needed help. Ruth would have said kindness mattered most when it was inconvenient. Ruth had been the kind of Christian who actually lived what she believed, inconvenient though it often was.

Ellie was fresh out of faith these days, but old habits died hard. And pride was a cold companion on a night like this.

"One night," she said finally, meeting his eyes. "Thank you."

Relief flickered across his face so fast she almost missed it—there and gone like a candle flame behind glass. He climbed out and came around to open her door before she could do it herself, the old-fashioned gesture so automatic she suspected he didn't even think about it anymore.

The wind snatched her breath as she stepped down, cold air filling her lungs like ice water. Caleb's hand settled at her elbow—steady, warm through two layers of coat—and she found herself grateful for the support. Her legs felt less stable than she wanted to admit.

They were halfway up the walk when the front door of the house next door banged open with enough force to rattle its wreaths. Mrs. Mabel Hensley appeared on the porch like a Christmas apparition made flesh—seventy-three years old, four-foot-eleven in her sensible shoes, and wearing a red sweater covered in appliqué reindeer that should have been tacky but somehow worked on her.

"Caleb Brennan, is that Ellie Freeman I see?" Her voice carried clear to the next county, possibly the next state. "Lord have mercy, girl, we thought you'd gone Hollywood on us forever!"

Ellie managed a weak wave, acutely aware that every house on the street probably had eyes on them now. "Hi, Mabel."

"You come straight over here when you're settled! I've got chili simmering and cornbread in the oven, and I want to hear every detail of that big-city life of yours." Her sharp eyes didn't miss the way Caleb's hand rested at Ellie's elbow, the protective stance of his body slightly in front of hers. Mabel's smile could have lit up the whole street. "Though looks like our sheriff's already decided you're under his protection."

Caleb muttered something under his breath that might have been a prayer for patience, or possibly divine intervention.

Mabel beamed with the satisfaction of a woman who'd been waiting twelve years for this particular Christmas miracle. "Noah, baby, bring that dog inside before he freezes his tail off! And Ellie, honey—" her voice softened genuinely "—welcome home. We've missed you."

The door shut with a cheerful slam that somehow managed to sound triumphant. Somewhere down the block, another neighbor flicked on their porch lights, and Ellie could swear she saw a curtain twitch at the Harrison house across the street.

She felt heat climb her neck despite the frigid temperature. "Does she still tell everyone everything?"

"Faster than the internet," Caleb confirmed, steering her up his own front steps with gentle insistence. "By morning the whole town will know you're here. By lunch they'll have picked out wedding venues for us and decided on a color scheme."

She stumbled slightly on the top step, her tired legs finally giving her trouble. His grip tightened immediately, keeping her upright with casual strength.

He gave a brief grin that didn't quite reach his eyes, like he was testing a joke he wasn't sure he should've made. "Joking," he said quietly—though the look he gave her suggested the thought hadn't surprised him nearly as much as it should have

He shifted his weight, creating space again, like he didn't trust himself to linger too long in the moment.

She looked up at him under the glow of his porch light, at the snow caught in his dark hair and the shadows under his eyes that spoke of too many long shifts and not enough sleep. His walnut-color eyes, when they met hers, held something she couldn't quite name—something that definitely didn't look like he was joking at all.

Inside, the house smelled like pine and cinnamon and something savory that made her stomach growl with sudden, fierce hunger. Noah's voice echoed from somewhere deeper in the house, probably the kitchen. "Daddy, I saved her the reindeer pancake with the most chocolate chips! It's in the fridge for tomorrow!"

Caleb held the door open, one hand on the frame. Snow swirled in around their boots, melting immediately on the warm hardwood floor. He looked at her for a long moment, his expression impossible to read.

"Last chance to change your mind," he said softly. "I can still call Pastor Mike, see if—"

"I'm not changing my mind." She didn't let herself think too hard about what she was agreeing to, what it might mean. "One night. Warm bed. Tomorrow we figure out the rest."

One night, Ellie told herself firmly as she stepped over the threshold.

The door closed behind her with the soft, decisive click of something that couldn't be undone—like a story that had already decided how it was going to end, whether the characters were ready or not.

Chapter 3

The Brennan house smelled like a Christmas card had exploded in the best possible way.

Pine dominated—from the ten-foot noble fir that took up half the living room, its branches full and fragrant in a way that only real trees could manage. Cinnamon wafted from the kitchen, probably from whatever was simmering on the stove in a slow cooker. And underneath it all was the faint, unmistakable scent of little-boy sneakers and wet dog that no amount of Febreze could completely conquer—not unpleasant, just honest.

Ellie stood dripping on the entry mat, suddenly afraid to move farther. It felt too intimate, too personal, being in Caleb Brennan's home. Seeing where he lived, where he ate breakfast and watched TV and tucked his son in at night. This was his private life, his sanctuary, and she was intruding.

Her gaze drifted instinctively, searching for signs of another woman—photos on the wall, shoes by the door, the quiet imprint of a wife's presence. The absence of it left her unsettled in a way she wasn't ready to name.

Caleb took her coat with the same quiet efficiency he'd used to wrap the blanket around her earlier, hanging it on a hook shaped like a cowboy boot. His own coat and hat followed, and without the bulk of winter gear, she could see he'd filled out since high school. Broader shoulders, thicker arms, the kind of solid strength that came from physical work and not just a gym. He moved with the easy confidence of a man comfortable in his own space.

Tripod shook snow from his fur in a full-body shimmy, splattering the log walls with melted slush. Then he flopped at Ellie's feet with a contented groan, as if he'd lived here his whole life and she was simply a long-awaited guest. His tail thumped against the floor in a rhythm that seemed to say *Finally, you're home.*

"Daddy, she's shivering!" Noah announced, appearing in the archway that led to what must be the kitchen. He wore an apron that read "Kiss the Cook—He's Tiny" in faded letters, clearly a hand-me-down from someone much larger. A streak of flour decorated one round cheek, and his hair stuck up in the back like he'd been running his hands through it. "I turned the guest room heater on high like you said."

"Good man." Caleb's mouth curved in something that wasn't quite a smile but came close, the kind of expression that transformed his whole face. "Ellie, boots off if you want. Floor's warm."

She toed off her soaked ankle boots—expensive leather ones from Los Angeles that were probably ruined now—and immediately curled her toes against radiant heat seeping through the hardwood. The warmth felt like pure luxury after the cold.

Noah grabbed her hand without asking permission, his small fingers sticky with what might have been cookie dough or possibly something else entirely. His grip was warm, certain, the unconscious trust of a child who'd been taught that adults were generally kind.

"Come see the tree! We waited for you."

"We did not," Caleb corrected, but his tone was mild, indulgent.

"We did in my heart," Noah insisted with the kind of logic that made perfect sense to eight-year-olds, tugging her forward with surprising strength.

The living room made her stop breathing for a second.

White lights twinkled through real pine needles, hundreds of them woven through the branches with care. A train set whistled around the base on a little track, the locomotive painted red and green, pulling cars loaded with tiny presents. Handmade ornaments covered every available branch—paper chains in construction paper, popsicle-stick stars held together with glue and hope, one very crooked clay handprint dated 2021 in a child's careful printing.

But it was the star at the top that made her throat tighten. She recognized it instantly—the same slightly lopsided star she remembered from high school, the one Caleb and his brothers had made in shop class the year their mom got sick. She'd been in study hall when she'd overheard him talking about it, his voice rough with emotion he was trying to hide. They'd made it together, the three Brennan boys, while their mother was in her final weeks of chemotherapy.

That he still had it, still used it, still placed it at the top of his tree where it could watch over everything—it said more about Caleb Brennan than a hundred conversations could.

Noah pointed proudly at the star, bouncing slightly on his toes. "Daddy lets me put the star up every year now. Mommy used to do it, but she's an angel in heaven, so she has better stars up there. Probably ones that don't lean to the left."

The words were matter-of-fact, delivered with the peculiar clarity that only children could manage when talking about death. There was sadness in them, but also acceptance. A child who'd learned to carry grief without letting it crush him.

The meaning landed slowly, then all at once.

Sarah was gone.

Not divorced. Not absent. Gone.

The knowledge hit Ellie with equal parts relief and shame—relief she hadn't earned, and shame for feeling it at all.

Ellie's throat closed completely. She couldn't have spoken if her life depended on it.

Caleb cleared it for her, his voice slightly rough. "Noah, go check the chili. Stir it three times clockwise, you know the rule. And don't add anything without asking first."

"But the marshmallows make it taste like winter!" Noah protested.

"Three times. Clockwise. Nothing added. Go."

Noah darted off toward the kitchen, Tripod scrambling after him with his peculiar three-legged gait that was surprisingly fast. The second they were gone, the room felt suddenly larger, quieter, more intimate.

Caleb watched her carefully, reading the shift in her expression the way he'd learned to read weather and witnesses alike. He knew that look—the moment when understanding rearranged everything. He didn't rush to fill the silence. Some truths needed space to breathe.

Caleb spoke low, his voice pitched for her ears only. "He does that. Talks about Sarah like she's just in the next room, like she might walk in any minute. His therapist says it's his way of keeping her close, that it's healthy. Most days I think she's right."

"It's sweet," Ellie managed, her voice barely above a whisper.

"It's complicated." He rubbed the back of his neck again, that telltale gesture she was beginning to recognize as his default when he was working through something difficult. "Some days it feels like healing. Other days it feels like we're both stuck. But he's eight, and he deserves to remember her however he needs to."

She wanted to say something comforting, something wise, but what did she know about loss like that? Her grandmother had died at eighty-three after a full life. Sad, yes, but expected. Natural. Not like losing a young wife, a mother, someone who should have had decades ahead of her.

"Guest room's upstairs, first door on the right," Caleb continued, shifting back to practical matters. "Towels are clean, changed them this morning. Bathroom's across the hall. I'll bring your bag up in a minute, let you get settled before supper."

She wanted to say she could get the bag herself, that she didn't need him waiting on her, but the truth was her legs felt like overcooked spaghetti. The adrenaline crash was hitting hard, leaving her shaky and exhausted.

"Thank you," she said instead. "For all of this. I know it's— I'm sure this isn't how you planned your evening."

"Ellie." He waited until she looked at him. "I pull people out of ditches for a living. Feed them, warm them up, make sure they're okay. That's the job. The difference is, most of them aren't—" He stopped, seemed to reconsider his words. "Most of them I don't remember from before. This is... different. But not bad different. Just different."

The heat in his gaze made her stomach flip in a way that had nothing to do with morning sickness.

She escaped to the stairs before she could do something stupid like ask what he meant by that. Her hand trailed along the smooth log railing as she climbed, the wood polished from years of use. Family photos lined the wall in mismatched frames that somehow worked together.

Caleb in uniform, impossibly young, holding a tiny Noah wrapped in a blue hospital blanket. Caleb and a pretty blonde woman laughing on a beach somewhere tropical, her hand on her pregnant belly, pure joy radiating from both their faces. Noah missing those same two front teeth, grinning beside a snowman wearing a sheriff's hat and badge. A family portrait taken at a studio, probably the last one before Sarah got sick—Noah couldn't have been more than six, still round-cheeked and baby-faced, sitting between his parents who looked at each other like they'd won the lottery.

Sarah had died five years ago—complications from a sudden illness that moved too fast and left no room for bargaining. One month she'd been tired. The next, she was gone. The kind of loss that didn't explode, just hollowed everything out and left the people behind figuring out how to live inside the echo.

The photos told a story of love and loss, of a family that had been complete and then wasn't, of the ones left behind trying to figure out how to keep going.

The guest room was small and perfect. A quilt in shades of blue and cream covered the bed, the pattern something traditional and hand-stitched. An iron bedframe that looked antique but sturdy. A dormer window already frosting at the edges, looking out over the snow-covered street. Simple furniture —a dresser, a nightstand, a rocking chair in the corner with a knitted throw draped over its arm.

But it was the little tabletop tree on the dresser that made her press a hand to her mouth. Someone—Noah, judging by the enthusiastic excess—had set up a miniature Christmas tree, complete with a single strand of colored lights and a construction-paper sign taped to the mirror behind it. The sign read WELCOME ELLIE in careful block letters, with stars drawn in each corner and what might have been an attempt at holly berries but looked more like red blobs.

She sat on the edge of the bed and pressed both hands to her face, trying to hold back tears that wanted to come anyway. When had anyone last made her feel welcome? When had anyone gone out of their way to make sure she felt like she belonged?

Mark certainly never had. In their five years of marriage, she'd always felt like a guest in her own home, walking on eggshells, trying to be the right kind of wife for a man who was never quite satisfied.

A soft knock at the doorframe. Caleb stood there with her duffel, his shoulder filling the frame. He took in the sign, the tree, her barely controlled tears, and pretended not to notice any of it—the mercy of someone who understood that sometimes people needed to fall apart without an audience.

"Chili's almost ready. Noah insists you have to taste it before he adds the—" he paused, clearly searching for patience "—the unicorn sparkles."

"Unicorn sparkles?" Ellie's voice came out watery, but at least she was smiling.

"Mini marshmallows. Don't ask." He set the bag down just inside the door, careful not to intrude further into the space. "Take your time. Bathroom's across the hall if you want to wash up or change or... whatever you need. No rush."

He started to leave, and she found herself not wanting him to go. Not wanting to be alone with her thoughts and her fears and the tiny life growing inside her that made everything feel both more urgent and more impossible.

"Caleb."

He paused in the doorway, turned back slightly.

"Thank you," she said again, knowing it wasn't enough but

not having better words. "I didn't say it earlier, not really. I was...
a mess. But thank you. For stopping. For helping. For this." She
gestured vaguely at the room, the tree, everything.

Something softened around his eyes, making him look
younger, more like the boy she'd known. "Anybody would've
done the same."

"No," she said quietly, with absolute certainty. "They
wouldn't have. Not like this."

For a moment the space between them felt charged, full of
things neither of them was quite ready to say. The air seemed to
thicken with possibility, with the weight of twelve years and all
the roads not taken.

Then Noah's voice floated up the stairs, breaking the
moment. "Daaaaaaad! The marshmallows are melting funny!
They're making shapes! Come see! This one looks like Tripod!"

Caleb's mouth twitched in what might have been
exasperation or amusement or both. "Duty calls. The
marshmallows wait for no man."

He tapped the doorframe twice—a casual gesture, the kind
you might make when leaving any room—and disappeared
down the hallway. She heard his footsteps on the stairs, heard
Noah's excited chatter rise to meet him, heard Tripod's single
bark of joy.

Ellie exhaled shakily and opened her duffel with hands that
trembled slightly. She pulled out clean clothes—soft yoga pants
and an oversized sweatshirt that hid the small swell of her belly.
Then she reached into the inner pocket and withdrew the one
thing she hadn't let the movers pack, the one thing she'd insisted
on carrying herself.

Grandma Ruth's old Bible.

The leather cover was soft as cloth, worn smooth by decades
of handling. The spine was cracked in multiple places, held
together more by habit than structure. Pages threatened to fall
out if you weren't careful. The margins were filled with Ruth's
handwriting—notes, prayers, dates marking significant
moments, cross-references connecting verses across testaments.

Ellie set it on the nightstand next to Noah's little tree and stared at it for a long minute. She hadn't opened it since the funeral. Hadn't been able to. Every page held Ruth's voice, Ruth's faith. Ruth had believed the world was held together by something good—something steady, something bigger than fear. Ellie wasn't sure she believed that anymore. But she wanted to.

Ellie wasn't sure she believed any of that anymore. Wasn't sure what she believed, if she was honest.

But Ruth had believed enough for both of them, once. Maybe that was worth something.

Downstairs, a little boy laughed with pure delight. A dog barked once, the sound muffled by distance and floorboards. Pans clattered in a kitchen where someone was making dinner, making a life, making do with what remained after loss.

A man's low voice rumbled something that might have been teasing or exasperation—she couldn't tell which—and Noah's giggles erupted like fireworks.

Ellie pressed a hand to the tiny curve of her belly, still hidden beneath loose clothes and careful posture. The baby gave a tiny flutter in response, as if to say *I'm here, I'm real, you're not alone.*

She whispered the first honest prayer she'd managed in months, her voice barely audible even to herself.

"Okay," she whispered into the quiet. "I don't know what I believe right now. But I'm listening."

She stopped, swallowed hard. What did she want?

A home. A family. A place to belong. All the things she'd thought she had in Nevada, until the illusion shattered like ice under too much weight.

Grandma Ruth's voice surfaced from memory, gentle but firm, warning her once—*Don't tie your life to someone who doesn't share your faith, Ellie. Love isn't enough if you're pulling in different directions.*

Ellie had rolled her eyes then. She wasn't rolling them now.

From the kitchen drifted the unmistakable sound of Caleb singing along to "Jingle Bell Rock" playing on a radio somewhere. He was off-key, quiet, utterly unselfconscious in a way that spoke of a man who didn't care if anyone heard him.

The sound made something in her chest crack open, just a little. Just enough to let in a sliver of light.

Ellie smiled despite herself, despite everything. She wiped her eyes, changed into her comfortable clothes, and went downstairs to taste chili with unicorn sparkles and pretend, just for one evening, that she was the kind of person who belonged in a warm kitchen with a ready-made family.

Just for tonight, she could pretend she'd come home instead of running away. Just for tonight.

Once, she'd believed leaving was the only way to become someone more. That staying meant settling.

Now she understood the truth she'd missed back then: places don't make you small. Fear does. And running from it only makes it louder.

Chapter 4

Supper was chaos in the very best way.

Noah insisted Ellie sit at the head of the table "because you're the guest of honor and Daddy says guests get the best seat," which meant Caleb had to scoot his chair sideways so Tripod could wedge his brindle bulk under the table and rest his head on Ellie's foot like a living, breathing slipper. The dog's warmth seeped through her thick socks, oddly comforting.

The chili was surprisingly good—Caleb had a heavier hand with cumin than she expected, and there was a depth of flavor that suggested he'd been making this recipe long enough to perfect it. The "unicorn sparkles" turned out to be mini marshmallows that Noah added with ceremonial precision, counting out exactly seven per bowl because "seven is God's favorite number, Mrs. Mabel says."

The marshmallows dissolved into sweet pockets of ridiculous joy, the sugar cutting through the heat of the spices in a way that shouldn't have worked but somehow did.

Conversation flowed the way only an eight-year-old can make it flow—chaotic, enthusiastic, veering wildly from topic to topic without warning or apparent logic.

"Do you have a job in the city?" Noah asked around a mouthful of cornbread, crumbs decorating his chin.

"Yes, marketing," Ellie answered, reaching for her water glass.

"That's like making commercials?"

"Sort of. I help companies figure out how to tell people about their products. What makes them special, why someone should buy them instead of something else."

Noah considered this with the seriousness of a child trying to understand adult concepts. "Do you know the guy who does the GEICO gecko?"

Ellie bit back a smile. "No, but I wish I did. That gecko's pretty famous."

Noah nodded solemnly, as if this were a tragic missed opportunity that might have changed the course of history. "I would ask him if he's really a gecko or just a guy in a gecko suit. Because the voice sounds like a guy."

"It is a guy," Caleb interjected, ladling more chili into Noah's bowl. "Voice actor. We've been through this."

"But how do you *know*?" Noah persisted with the philosophical determination of someone not willing to let facts get in the way of wonder. "Have you *seen* him? What if he's secretly a real gecko who learned to talk and nobody knows?"

Caleb shot Ellie a look that said *This is my life now. This is what I deal with.*

She smiled despite the exhaustion pulling at her bones, despite the surreal situation, despite everything. "I think you might have uncovered a conspiracy, Noah."

Noah beamed at her like she'd given him the greatest gift imaginable. "Daddy says my brain works in mysterious ways."

"Your teacher says that too," Caleb muttered. "Usually right before she suggests we 'channel all that energy into something productive.'"

"I *am* productive. I made a volcano last week that erupted *real* lava."

"It was baking soda and vinegar."

"It looked like lava. Jake Hensley said it was the best volcano in the whole third grade."

Caleb refilled Ellie's bowl without asking, the gesture automatic, attentive in a way that made her hyperaware of him. Every time their fingers brushed—his passing the cornbread, hers reaching for the butter—she felt it like a spark of static electricity. The shock of contact, brief and electric.

After the third helping of unicorn sparkles and two pieces of cornbread that Ellie didn't remember eating, Noah yawned so wide his eyes watered. His head started to droop toward his bowl before Caleb caught him.

"Bedtime, buddy."

"One more chapter of the reindeer book!" Noah pleaded, suddenly wide awake with the miraculous energy reserves that children possessed when bedtime loomed. "Ellie hasn't heard how Rudolph saves Christmas yet!"

Ellie opened her mouth to say she didn't mind, that she could handle one children's book, but Caleb was already standing, his hand gentle on Noah's shoulder.

"Tomorrow night. Guest of honor gets to pick the book tomorrow, remember?" He looked at Ellie, something uncertain in his expression. Something in his look made her wonder if he was already bracing for goodbye. As if he knew—better than she did—that nothing about her life stayed simple for long.

"You mind helping with bedtime? He'll be impossible otherwise. He'll spend the next hour trying to sneak downstairs to show you his rock collection or explain his theory about whether Santa uses GPS or magic to navigate."

She minded very much and not at all. The intimacy of bedtime routines, of tucking in a child, felt like crossing another invisible line. But Noah was already looking at her with such hopeful expectation that she couldn't possibly refuse.

"Lead the way."

Noah's room was a shrine to all things eight-year-old boy. Dinosaur sheets that had probably been cool two years ago. A constellation projector glowing softly on the dresser, casting slow-moving stars across the ceiling in mesmerizing patterns. Enough LEGOs scattered across the floor to constitute a legitimate public safety hazard—Ellie stepped carefully, remembering the unique agony of stepping on a LEGO brick barefoot.

Bookshelves lined one wall, packed with everything from board books clearly outgrown but kept anyway, to chapter books with cracked spines from multiple readings. A desk held school papers, art projects, and what looked like an ambitious attempt at building a catapult from popsicle sticks.

But it was the framed photo on the dresser that made Ellie's breath catch. A smiling blonde woman—Sarah—laughing at the camera with her whole face, one hand resting on a very pregnant belly. She wore a sundress and stood in front of this very house, the Victorian's wraparound porch visible behind her. The love and joy radiating from that single image was almost tangible.

Noah dove under the covers fully clothed, still wearing his flour-dusted shirt and jeans. Caleb peeled him out again with the practiced efficiency of someone who'd fought this battle nightly, stripping him down to his underwear while Noah protested that "cavemen slept in their clothes."

"Cavemen didn't have washing machines," Caleb countered. "Pajamas. Now."

Noah wriggled into reindeer flannel that looked soft from many washings, then patted the bed on either side with both hands. "One chapter. Daddy does the voices, Ellie does the sound effects."

They settled on either side of him—Caleb on the left, Ellie on the right, Noah in the middle like the point of connection between them. The bed was a full size, just barely big enough for three if everyone stayed close. Ellie could feel the heat of Caleb's body across the small space, separated by eight-year-old boy and two thin blankets.

Ellie stayed very still, afraid that if she relaxed too much she might forget this wasn't her place. That this wasn't her life. It was only a borrowed moment, fragile as glass.

The book was well-worn, pages soft from countless readings. *Rudy the Reindeer Who Could Talk to Snowflakes*. Caleb opened it with the reverence of someone handling a treasured possession.

He read about a reindeer who felt different from all the others because he could hear what the snowflakes were saying as they fell. His grumpy-elf voice was surprisingly excellent— gravelly and annoyed in all the right places. The snowflake voices were high and tinkly. The other reindeer sounded properly skeptical.

When it was Ellie's turn for sound effects—wind howling

through a winter storm—she did her best, though she suspected she sounded more like a broken furnace than atmospheric weather. Noah applauded anyway, his small hands clapping with genuine enthusiasm.

Tripod sprawled across the foot of the bed, snoring before they reached page three, his single back leg twitching occasionally as he chased dream rabbits.

The story unfolded exactly as countless Christmas stories did —the different one saving the day, being celebrated for his uniqueness, learning that what made him strange was actually what made him special. Simple, predictable, and somehow perfect in its simplicity.

When Caleb turned the last page, Noah's eyes were heavy, fighting to stay open despite his best efforts.

"Prayer," Noah mumbled, his voice thick with approaching sleep.

Caleb bowed his head automatically, the motion so ingrained it was clearly habit. Ellie froze, uncertain. She hadn't prayed out loud with anyone in years. Hadn't known what to say, how to form the words. Private whispered pleas were one thing. Public prayer felt like exposure.

Noah didn't notice her hesitation. He folded his small hands together and started speaking, his voice soft and sincere.

"Dear God, thank You for chili and unicorn sparkles and for sending Ellie even though her car went whoosh into the ditch." He paused for a breath. "Please help Tripod grow his leg back, or at least find one he likes better. Maybe a robot one like in that movie. And please let Daddy smile more because he has a really good smile when he forgets to be sad. Help him remember Mommy's happy and not hurting anymore. And help Ellie not be scared, because she looks scared sometimes when she thinks nobody's watching—and You always are. Amen."

Ellie's heart cracked right down the middle, splitting like ice under pressure. Tears burned behind her eyes and she had to look away, focusing on the constellation projector to keep from breaking down completely.

It wasn't the prayer itself that undid her—it was the certainty behind it. The uncomplicated belief that people mattered, that fear could be named, that love was worth asking for out loud.

Caleb's voice was rough when he added, "Amen." He didn't look at her right away. When he finally did, it was careful—like he was deliberately choosing distance instead of the pull between them.

He tucked the blankets tight around Noah with practiced motions, smoothing them down, making sure no cold air could sneak in. Then he leaned down and kissed Noah's forehead, his lips lingering there a moment longer than necessary.

"Love you, bud. Sleep good."

"Love you too, Daddy." Noah's eyes were already closing. "Love you, Ellie."

The words were drowsy, probably automatic, the kind of thing he said to everyone at bedtime. But they still hit her like a physical blow. She managed to whisper, "Love you too, Noah," before her throat closed completely.

Caleb flicked off the light. The constellation projector painted slow-moving stars across the ceiling, familiar constellations rendered in soft blue light. Orion. The Big Dipper. Cassiopeia. The same stars people had been looking at for thousands of years, constant and unchanging.

In the hallway, the silence felt suddenly huge, pressing in from all sides.

Ellie hugged herself, wrapping her arms around her middle. "He's... incredible."

"Yeah." Caleb rubbed the back of his neck, the gesture automatic now. "He gets that from his mom. The big heart, the way he sees people. That's all Sarah."

It isn't all Sarah, Ellie wanted to say. *It's you, too.* The patience. The steadiness. The way love seemed to radiate from him without effort.

Caleb had never been the kind of man who talked about what he believed. He lived it quietly, the way his father had taught him—by showing up when it mattered.

They stood there in the dim hallway, two feet apart, the soft glow from Noah's night-light spilling between them in a wedge of pale illumination. Somewhere downstairs, the grandfather clock in the living room ticked steadily. Outside, wind rattled the windows, carrying more snow.

It would have taken one step. One careless breath. Ellie felt the weight of that choice settle between them—and the quiet relief that neither of them made it.

Finally Caleb spoke, his voice low and careful. "You don't have to do this, Ellie. Stay, I mean. I can call Pastor Mike, see if the parsonage is open—"

"I'm not afraid of children, Caleb." She tried for a smile, tried to inject some lightness into the heavy moment. "Or dogs. Or unicorn marshmallows. Or eight-year-olds who pray for robot legs and less sad daddies."

His eyes searched hers in the dim light, looking for something. "It's not the kid or the dog I'm worried about."

The air thinned between them. She knew exactly what he meant—could feel it in the way her pulse kicked up, in the hyperawareness of how close he was standing, in the memory of his hands gentle on her shoulders, his voice steady in the storm.

This—whatever it was building between them—that was what he was worried about.

They'd never really ended—just missed their chance. Timing, fear, ambition pulling them in opposite directions. She'd wanted out of this town before it decided her life for her. He'd been rooted here, already carrying responsibilities she hadn't been brave enough to share.

Downstairs, the grandfather clock chimed nine times, each note clear and resonant. Tripod's snores drifted up from Noah's room, punctuated by the occasional dream-whimper.

Ellie broke first, taking a step back—not because she didn't want him close, but because she wanted him to still be standing there tomorrow. "I should... shower. Long day. Very long day."

"Right." He stepped back too, hands sliding into his pockets like he didn't trust them otherwise. "Towels are in the hall closet, should be some on the top shelf. Hot water takes a minute to wake up, so give it time before you give up on it."

She nodded, escaping toward the bathroom before she could do something stupid. Before she could ask what he'd been about to say. Before she could let herself want things that were too complicated, too impossible.

She closed the bathroom door and leaned against it, eyes squeezed shut, breathing hard like she'd run a race.

Get a grip, Freeman. One night. Warm bed. Nothing more.

But when she opened her eyes, the mirror showed a woman with flushed cheeks and snow-damp hair starting to dry in messy waves. A woman with shadows under her eyes and a secret growing beneath her ribs that suddenly felt too big for one person to carry alone.

A woman who looked terrifyingly close to hoping for something she shouldn't want.

She turned on the shower and let the steam swallow her whole, let the hot water beat against her shoulders and wash away the grime of the road, the shock of the accident, the weight of the day. But it couldn't wash away the memory of Caleb's hands gentle on her shoulders, or Noah's prayer for her not to be scared, or the way this house had felt more like home in three hours than her house in Las Vegas had felt in three years.

Across the hall, in the dark, Caleb stood outside Noah's door a long time, listening to his son breathe. The steady in-out that meant deep sleep, the kind of rest only children could achieve.

Then he looked toward the bathroom door where light seeped under the bottom crack and water ran steady and warm. Where Ellie Freeman—the girl who'd tutored him in study hall, who'd smiled at him in ways that made his teenage heart stutter, who'd left for college and never looked back—was washing away the day.

She'd come back. After twelve years, she'd come back.

And she was in trouble. He could see it in the shadows under her eyes, in the way she'd flinched when Noah asked about her job, in the careful way she held herself like she was protecting something precious. In the way she'd gone very still when he'd mentioned her ex's name this afternoon, like just hearing it caused pain.

He whispered one word into the quiet hallway, so low no one could have heard it even if they'd been standing right next to him.

"Sarah."

It wasn't a prayer exactly, more of an acknowledgment. A question posed to someone who couldn't answer. *What do I do with this? What do I do with her? With these feelings that have no business existing?*

The silence gave him no answers.

Then, louder, to the empty hallway and maybe to God if He was listening: "Lord, I'm gonna need a bigger miracle than snow tires this time. Because I'm already in over my head, and she hasn't even been here four hours."

He went downstairs to lie on the couch that was suddenly six inches too short, his feet hanging off the end. Habit more than courtesy—since Sarah's death, the couch had been where he landed whenever his thoughts got too loud. He lay there staring at the ceiling, at the colored lights from the Christmas tree casting shadows that danced and shifted.

He pretended he wasn't already in over his head. Wanting her was easy. Being worthy of her—that was the harder thing. And tonight, restraint felt like the only honest choice.

He pretended his heart wasn't doing dangerous things every time Ellie Freeman smiled.

He pretended tomorrow would bring clarity instead of complications.

He lay there staring at the ceiling, fully aware that pretending wasn't going to save him.

But late into the night, as snow continued to fall and bury the roads deeper, Caleb Brennan lay awake and admitted to himself what he'd been trying to deny since the moment he'd seen her standing by that wrecked SUV.

He was in trouble.
The best kind of trouble.
and the worst.
And he had no idea what to do about it.

Chapter 5

Ellie woke to the smell of coffee and the unmistakable sound of a small boy trying—and failing spectacularly—to be quiet.

She lay still for a moment, cataloguing the unfamiliar sensations. Soft quilt against her cheek, warm and heavy in a way hotel blankets never were. The faint glow of Christmas lights bleeding through curtains that weren't quite thick enough to block them out. The muted thud of someone attempting to tiptoe past her door in cowboy boots that were clearly several sizes too big, each step accompanied by a scuffing sound that defeated the entire purpose of tiptoeing.

A dog sighed in his sleep somewhere down the hall, a long, contented exhale that spoke of dreams and full bellies.

For one disorienting second she forgot where she was, her sleep-fogged brain scrambling to place the sounds and smells. Then memory slammed back with the force of a freight train: the ditch, the accident, Caleb's hands steady on her shoulders, Noah's prayer about his daddy's smile and her being scared.

The baby gave a tiny flutter low in her belly, as if reminding her that nothing in her life was simple anymore. As if she could forget. The doctor had laughed and called it gas, but Ellie knew better. Whatever the medical explanation, this felt intentional— like a tiny reminder tapping from the inside.

She sat up slowly, her body cataloguing new aches. Her shoulder where the seatbelt had caught. Her lower back from the impact. Nothing serious, nothing that wouldn't fade in a day or two, but enough to remind her how much worse it could have been.

The little tabletop tree blinked its cheerful pattern—red-green-red-green—in the gray morning light filtering through the window. Someone had come in while she slept. Her clothes from yesterday, which she'd left draped over the rocking chair, were now folded neatly on the dresser. Her boots, soaked and ruined from the snow, had been lined up beneath the window, stuffed with newspaper to help them dry and keep their shape.

A note in bold, slanted handwriting lay on top of the folded clothes, the letters pressed deep into the paper like the writer had a heavy hand:

Tow truck's coming at nine. Coffee's on. Help yourself to anything in the kitchen. Noah already asked if you like scrambled or fried. I told him to wait and ask you himself. —C

Short, practical, and still somehow gentle in its efficiency. She traced the single letter signature with one finger, then felt ridiculous for the flutter it caused in her chest and made herself stop.

She got dressed in fresh clothes—jeans and a soft gray sweater that camouflaged the small bump, though she was starting to wonder how much longer she could hide it. At thirteen weeks, she was entering that awkward phase where she just looked like she'd been enjoying too many donuts, not quite obviously pregnant but not quite her normal shape either.

Downstairs, the kitchen was warm and bright with morning sun streaming through windows that faced east. Caleb stood at the stove flipping pancakes with the focused attention of someone who took breakfast seriously. He'd changed from yesterday's uniform into jeans and a dark green henley, the sleeves pushed up to reveal forearms dusted with flour. His hair was slightly damp, like he'd showered recently, and he hadn't shaved yet—dark stubble shadowed his jaw.

Noah sat at the table coloring a picture with intense concentration, his tongue sticking out the corner of his mouth the way children did when they were focused. The drawing appeared to be Tripod wearing a superhero cape and flying through the air, all three legs extended in dynamic action poses.

The dog himself was sprawled across the threshold between the kitchen and living room like a speed bump with opinions, his body positioned perfectly to trip anyone who wasn't paying attention.

"Morning," Ellie said softly, not wanting to startle anyone.

Both males looked up at once, their heads swiveling in perfect synchronization. Noah's grin threatened to split his face in half, pure joy radiating from every pore. Caleb's expression did something complicated—surprise, pleasure, something warmer that he quickly shuttered—before settling into careful neutrality.

"Morning," Caleb returned, his voice still rough with early morning. "Sleep okay?"

"Like the dead. Your guest bed is unfairly comfortable." She moved into the kitchen, drawn by the smell of coffee like a moth to flame.

He shrugged, flipping a perfect golden pancake with practiced ease. "Sarah picked it out. Said if we were gonna have company, they deserved better than my old army cot and a sleeping bag."

The casual mention of his wife's name hung in the air for half a second. Ellie watched Caleb's face carefully, but there was no pain there, no flinching. Just matter-of-fact acknowledgment, the way you'd mention anyone who'd influenced a decision.

She decided not to dance around it, not to pretend the woman in the photographs didn't exist. "She had excellent taste."

Something in his shoulders relaxed, like she'd passed a test she hadn't known she was taking. "She did. In most things." His mouth quirked slightly. "Questionable taste in husbands, though."

"Daddy!" Noah looked up from his drawing, scandalized. "Mommy said you were the handsomest man in all of Colorado. She wrote it in her journal. I read it when we got her memory box down."

Caleb's ears turned slightly red. "That's private, bud."

"But it's true! She drew a heart and everything!"

Ellie bit back a smile and slid into the chair Noah was patting enthusiastically with one flour-dusted hand. "What are you drawing?"

"It's Tripod saving Christmas! See, he's flying to catch Santa's sleigh before it crashes into the mountain because the reindeer all got food poisoning from eating bad carrots." Noah pointed to various elements of his drawing with the authority of someone who'd thought this through. "This is the explosion. This is Tripod's cape. This is Santa saying 'thank you, Tripod, you're the best dog ever.'"

"It's very dramatic," Ellie said seriously.

"Mrs. Patterson says I have a flair for drama. I looked up 'flair' and it means I'm good at making things exciting."

"That's one interpretation," Caleb muttered, setting a plate in front of Ellie.

The pancake had an ambitious number of antlers protruding from what was presumably a reindeer's head, plus what might have been eyes or might have been chocolate chips—it was hard to tell. Ellie took a bite and made appropriate appreciative noises, the pancake fluffy and sweet and exactly what she needed.

Caleb set a mug of coffee beside her—black with two sugars, exactly how she'd drunk it in high school study hall when she'd tutored him in algebra. When she'd sit across from him at those scarred library tables, trying not to stare at the way his brow furrowed when he was concentrating, trying to focus on quadratic equations instead of the way his hand moved across the page.

Back then, she'd told herself silence was maturity. That wanting more than Estrella Ridge made her practical, not cruel. She'd been proud—too proud to admit she cared more than she should, too afraid of how small her dreams might look if she anchored them to a boy who loved this place enough to stay. Caleb had always been rooted here, steady as the mountains. And Ellie had been desperate to prove she wasn't.

So she'd left with her feelings neatly folded away, convincing herself that some things were better unsaid than chosen.

She raised an eyebrow at the perfectly prepared coffee.

He lifted one shoulder, a half-shrug that tried to be casual and failed. "Good memory for useless details."

"Remembering how someone takes their coffee after twelve

years isn't useless," she said softly.

His eyes met hers for a long moment, something passing between them that made her pulse quicken. Then Noah launched into a detailed explanation of how Tripod had tried to help make pancakes by standing on his back leg and reaching for the mixing bowl, and the moment fractured into the comfortable chaos of morning.

Ellie let the chatter wash over her, warm and easy. Caleb moved around the kitchen with quiet efficiency—refilling Noah's milk before the glass was empty, nudging Tripod out from underfoot with one socked foot, checking his phone when it buzzed but not responding to whatever message had come through.

It felt dangerously domestic. Like she belonged here. Like this was her kitchen, her family, her morning routine.

Like she had any right to those feelings after being here less than twenty-four hours.

The doorbell rang, cutting through the breakfast coziness. Caleb wiped his hands on a dish towel decorated with dancing snowmen. "That'll be Hank with the tow truck."

Ellie stood too quickly, forgetting about the vertigo that sometimes hit her in the mornings now. The room tilted sideways for a second, gravity pulling in weird directions. She grabbed the back of the chair to steady herself.

Caleb's hand shot out to steady her elbow, his grip warm and solid. "You okay?"

"Fine. Just stood up too fast." She tried for a reassuring smile, but his eyes had narrowed slightly, studying her with the focused attention of someone who noticed details for a living.

"Ellie—"

"I'm fine," she repeated, more firmly this time. "Really."

He looked like he wanted to argue, but the doorbell rang again, more insistent. He released her elbow reluctantly. "Stay put. Finish your breakfast. I'll handle Hank."

He disappeared toward the front door, and Ellie sank back into her chair, heart pounding harder than the minor dizzy spell warranted. Noah leaned across the table conspiratorially, his voice dropping to what he probably thought was a whisper but was actually perfectly audible.

"Daddy likes you," he stage-whispered, loud enough to be heard in the next county.

Ellie choked on her coffee, coughing hard enough to make her eyes water.

Noah patted her arm sympathetically. "It's okay. Daddy says I have no indoor voice. But it's still true. He made the special pancakes. He only makes those for people he really likes."

"Noah—"

"And he put on the nice shirt. The green one Aunt Rachel gave him for his birthday that he says is too fancy for regular days. And he checked his hair in the bathroom mirror twice. I heard him."

"Maybe we should—"

"And last night after you went to bed, he lay on the couch for a really long time just staring at the Christmas tree, and when I came down for water he said he was praying, but I think he was thinking about you because—"

"Noah James Brennan." Caleb's voice came from the doorway, not quite sharp but carrying a clear warning. "Are you sharing private information again?"

Noah looked entirely unrepentant. "I'm being helpful. Mrs. Mabel says grown-ups are bad at talking about feelings and sometimes need help."

"Mrs. Mabel," Caleb said with the patience of a man who'd had this conversation before, "needs to mind her own business."

"She says that's impossible in a small town."

Caleb pinched the bridge of his nose, taking a moment to gather himself. When he opened his eyes, he looked directly at Ellie with an expression that was equal parts apology and resignation.

"I have good news and bad news."

Ellie set down her coffee mug carefully. "Bad news first. Always bad news first."

"Your SUV's not going anywhere till the shop gets a new radiator shipped in. Might be Wednesday. Maybe Thursday if the parts supplier is slow."

She closed her eyes, feeling the last threads of her carefully maintained control starting to fray. "Of course it is."

"Good news," he continued, his voice gentle, "Hank says the ditch cushioned the worst of it. Frame's fine. Could have been much worse. And—" he paused, and she could hear the careful diplomacy in his tone "—I went ahead and checked on Ruth's place while you were sleeping. The furnace is definitely frozen, and the pipes are too. Plumber took one look and said he can't get to it till after New Year's. He's backed up with emergency calls from people whose heat actually works but needs repair."

Ellie felt the walls of the cozy kitchen tilt inward, the space suddenly too small. "So I'm... stuck. Here. In Estrella Ridge."

"Looks like." He hesitated, his weight shifting like he was uncomfortable. "Spare room's still yours as long as you need it. I mean, if you want. No pressure. But the offer stands."

Noah bounced in his seat with barely contained excitement. "Yes! Tripod, did you hear? Ellie's staying!"

Tripod lifted his head from where he'd been dozing, thumped his tail twice in approval, then went back to sleep.

Ellie opened her mouth to protest—she had a life, a job she'd taken leave from, a doctor's appointment in Las Vegas on Tuesday that she couldn't miss. But the words wouldn't come. The truth was, the idea of driving back over the pass right now made her stomach lurch worse than morning sickness ever had. And where would she go? Back to her empty apartment? To the job she'd been avoiding? To the life that had fallen apart?

Caleb watched her face, reading the parade of emotions she couldn't quite hide. "No pressure," he repeated. "I can put you on the shuttle to Durango if you really need to go. Runs twice a day, weather permitting. Or you can stay. Whatever you need."

She looked at Noah's hopeful gap-toothed grin, at Tripod's crooked adoration, at Caleb standing there with flour on his sleeve and quiet patience in his storm-gray eyes. At this kitchen that smelled like coffee and pancakes and the kind of home she'd been dreaming about since long before she'd married the wrong man.

"I'll stay," she said, the words coming out more firmly than she felt. "A few days. Until the car's fixed. If you're sure I'm not imposing."

"Imposing?" Noah looked confused. "What's imposing?"

"It means being a bother," Ellie explained.

"You're not a bother! You're the best thing that happened all week! Except for when I found that really cool rock that looks like a dinosaur egg, but you're definitely number two!"

Caleb's smile was small and crooked and did something devastating to Ellie's heartbeat. "Welcome to the chaos, then. Fair warning—it doesn't get calmer from here."

Outside, the snow kept falling, soft and relentless, erasing every track that led away from Estrella Ridge. The pass would be closed for hours, maybe days. The roads were impassable. The weather was conspiring.

Or maybe, Ellie thought as she watched Noah show Caleb his drawing and Caleb ruffle his son's hair with such casual affection it made her chest ache—maybe this wasn't conspiracy.

Maybe this was providence.

She pressed a hand to her belly under the table where no one could see, and the baby fluttered in response like a tiny fist bump of agreement.

Okay, she thought. *Okay. We're staying. Just for a few days. Just until we figure out what comes next.*

But even as she thought it, part of her knew she was lying to herself.

Because Estrella Ridge had a way of keeping what it claimed.

And Caleb Brennan had a way of looking at her that made her want to be kept.

Chapter 6

By noon the entire town knew Ellie Freeman was staying at Caleb Brennan's house.

Mabel Hensley had apparently appointed herself town crier, because when Caleb dropped Ellie at Grandma Ruth's place to sort through what could be salvaged, three church ladies were already on the porch with casseroles, measuring tapes, and the kind of determined expressions that suggested they'd come prepared for battle with frozen pipes and possibly demons.

"We heard about the furnace," declared Mrs. Patterson, who'd taught Sunday school since approximately the Eisenhower administration. She thrust a foil-covered dish into Ellie's hands with the force of someone making a delivery that could not be refused. "Green bean casserole. Your grandmother's recipe. I got it from her before she passed. God rest her soul."

"And we brought thermometers," added Carol Jean Martinez, who ran the flower shop and apparently also dabbled in home inspection. She brandished a digital temperature reader like a weapon. "In case the pipes burst worse than we thought. Prevention is cheaper than cure, that's what my daddy always said."

Ellie accepted the foil-covered pan—funeral potatoes, because apparently that was the universal welcome-back-to-town dish, regardless of whether anyone had actually died—and tried to look grateful instead of cornered.

"That's very kind of you all, but I'm not sure—"

"Nonsense!" Mabel appeared behind the other two women like a general surveying her troops, her red sweater today featuring appliquéd reindeer that appeared to be wearing sunglasses. "We're putting you on the Christmas on the Square committee. Your fancy marketing degree is exactly what this festival needs. Last year the youth group tried to make the live nativity 'edgy.' The donkey wore sunglasses and a leather jacket.

Pastor Mike nearly had a stroke."

"I'm not sure I'm qualified—"

"You sold things for a living in the city, didn't you?" Mabel didn't wait for an answer. "Then you're qualified. First meeting's tomorrow at three. Courthouse meeting room. Don't be late."

Ellie opened her mouth to protest, caught sight of three pairs of eyes staring at her with the implacable determination of church ladies on a mission, and decided resistance was futile. "Of course. Three o'clock. I'll be there."

Caleb, traitor that he was, just tipped his hat and backed toward his truck with barely concealed amusement dancing in his eyes. "Call if you need anything. I've got a thing at the office, but I'll be back by three to pick you up."

"Coward," she mouthed at him.

His grin was unrepentant. "Part of the job description. Self-preservation in the face of church ladies." He climbed into his truck and escaped before she could throw the funeral potatoes at him.

By three o'clock, Ellie had:

- Filled four industrial-sized trash bags with spoiled food from a refrigerator that smelled like regret and science experiments gone wrong
- Discovered the furnace was indeed dead as disco, possibly deader
- Been measured for an angel costume "just in case we need you for the nativity tableaux"
- Been assigned to co-chair the festival with Mabel because apparently "no" was not in the Estrella Ridge vocabulary
- Found Ruth's old recipe box and cried over handwritten cards in her grandmother's looping script
- Discovered a box of Christmas ornaments in the attic that made her cry harder
- And fielded approximately seventeen questions about whether she was "back for good" in a tone that suggested the questioners already knew the answer

She was on her knees in the dining room, wrapping Grandma Ruth's nativity figurines in newspaper—the same set that had sat on this sideboard every Christmas of her childhood—when her phone finally caught one bar of service. The device came alive with a series of aggressive buzzes, messages downloading in rapid succession.

Three missed calls. All from Mark.

Her stomach dropped like a stone thrown from a bridge.

Two voicemails. Both from Mark.

Four text messages, each one progressively more insistent:

We need to talk.

Ellie, this is ridiculous. Call me back.

I know you're screening my calls.

She stared at the screen until it went dark, her reflection ghostlike in the black glass. Then she shoved it back in her pocket and returned to wrapping the ceramic figures with hands that trembled slightly.

Not today. She couldn't deal with Mark today. Couldn't deal with his demands, his manipulation, his sudden need to reassert control now that she'd stopped responding—now that she'd chosen something he hadn't approved. Three months ago, he'd been perfectly clear that children were "not part of the plan," that her pregnancy was an inconvenience he wanted erased, not a responsibility he intended to claim. What he wanted now wasn't a child. It was leverage.

The front door creaked open without a knock—small town rules, where locked doors were more suggestion than requirement. Caleb's voice carried down the hall, warm and familiar.

"Ellie? You decent?"

"In here," she called, grateful her voice came out steadier than she felt.

He appeared in the doorway of the dining room, snow dusting his shoulders again despite the sun that had broken through the clouds an hour ago. He carried two paper cups from the diner, steam rising from the lids. "Peace offering. Figured you could use this after a morning with the church lady brigade."

"Mabel's terrifyingly efficient." She accepted the cup he offered—hot chocolate, she discovered when she sipped it, with extra whipped cream and a hint of peppermint. Exactly right, though she didn't remember telling him she liked peppermint.

"Always has been." He crouched beside her, his knees popping slightly with the motion, surveying the half-packed box of nativity figures with the careful attention he probably gave crime scenes. "Thought you could use backup. And maybe lunch. I brought sandwiches. They're in the truck."

She wrapped both hands around the cup like a lifeline, letting the warmth seep into her cold fingers. "Thank you. For everything. I keep saying that, don't I?"

"Stop, or I'll start charging rent." He picked up the newspaper-wrapped shepherd she'd just set down, turned it over gently in his large hands. "Ruth loved this set. Used to let me play with it when I mowed her lawn in high school. Paid me twenty bucks a week and lemonade. Told me the sheep were unionized and refused to work overtime."

Ellie laughed despite everything, the sound surprising her with its genuine warmth. "She told me the wise men were late because they stopped for coffee and got into a theological argument at the gas station about the difference between signs and wonders."

"Sounds like Ruth." He smiled, small and fond. "She had a way of making everything into a story. Made the whole Bible feel more real somehow, like these were actual people who had bad days and made stupid choices, not just stained-glass saints."

They worked in companionable quiet for a while, wrapping decades of memories in last week's headlines. The Estrella Ridge Gazette, full of local news—the high school basketball team's winning streak, announcements for the Christmas festival, obituaries for people whose names Ellie half-remembered.

When they reached the angel with the chipped wing—the one that had sat at the very top of Ruth's display, surveying the whole scene—Caleb held it up to the light streaming through the dining room window.

"Noah broke this," he said quietly, "the Christmas Sarah died. He was three, barely understood what 'gone' meant. Thought if he put the angel on the fridge, she could fly down to heaven and bring Mommy back. Knocked it clean off the mantel reaching for it.

Ruth had been staying with them then—bringing meals, sitting up through the long nights when sleep wouldn't come, refusing to let grief turn the house hollow. She heard the crash and came running. Found Noah sitting in the pieces, crying his heart out.

Ellie's fingers stilled on the baby Jesus she'd been wrapping. Her throat tightened.

"Ruth glued it back together," Caleb continued, his voice soft with memory. "Right there at her kitchen table. Took her an hour, maybe more. Let Noah help, even though his three-year-old hands weren't much use. When she finished, she told him angels don't need perfect wings to get where they're going. Told him his mama was already where she needed to be, whole and perfect and not hurting anymore. That the chipped wing was a reminder that broken things could still be beautiful."

He set the angel carefully in the box, cushioning it with extra newspaper. "Noah still believes that. That broken things can be beautiful. That's Ruth's gift to him. Maybe her gift to both of us."

She swallowed hard against the emotion threatening to spill over. "He still believes a lot of things. Faith like that—it's rare."

"Kid's got more faith in his pinky than I've got in my whole body some days." Caleb's eyes met hers, and there was something raw in them, something honest and unguarded. "You okay, Ellie? And I don't mean the 'I'm fine' kind of okay. I mean really okay."

The question was gentle, but his eyes saw too much. Saw past the careful walls she'd constructed, past the brave face she'd been wearing since Nevada.

She opened her mouth to lie—to say she was fine, always fine, everything was under control. But what came out instead was, "My ex has called three times today."

Caleb went very still, the kind of stillness that came before action. "Yeah?"

"I haven't answered." She said it quickly, needing him to know. "I blocked his number months ago, but he got a new one. I don't want to talk to him. I don't want to hear his voice or his excuses."

"Good." The single word carried weight, approval and something fiercer.

"I just—" She set down the figure she'd been holding, pressed both hands to her face. "I keep waiting for the guilt to hit. Or the panic. Or something. He was my husband for five years. I should feel something, right? But instead I just feel... relieved? Is that terrible?"

"No." Caleb shifted closer, close enough that she could smell coffee and winter air on him. "That's honest. And honest is better than guilty any day."

They packed the last figurine—baby Jesus, perpetually serene in his manger—and Caleb sealed the box with packing tape, his movements efficient and sure. The silence stretched between them, but it wasn't uncomfortable. Just full. Weighted with things that didn't need to be said out loud to be understood.

Finally Caleb stood, offered her a hand up. His palm was warm and calloused when her fingers met his, the grip strong without being overwhelming. "Come on. Let's get out of this mausoleum for a bit. I know a place."

She took his hand and let him pull her to her feet. "Where are we going?"

"Somewhere Ruth always said fixed everything that was broken." His smile was crooked, boyish. "Trust me?"

She did. That was the terrifying part.

Noah was at a birthday party across town—his first solo skating-free Saturday in weeks—having been loudly offended that "grown-ups ruin racing speed anyway."

Twenty minutes later they were parked at the edge of Miller's Pond, boots crunching through fresh powder toward the old ice-skating rink the town flooded every December. The warming hut was lit from within, strings of Christmas lights reflecting off the ice like scattered stars across a frozen sky. The ice itself was pristine, unmarked except for the grooves left by the zamboni that the volunteer fire department ran every morning.

Caleb carried two pairs of skates over his shoulder like it was the most natural thing in the world, like he'd planned this. Maybe he had.

"You remembered," Ellie whispered, something in her chest cracking open.

"That you could skate circles around me in high school?" His grin was warm, teasing. "Hard to forget the girl who lapped me while humming 'Jingle Bells' backwards and never breaking a sweat. Pretty sure you're still the reason I have performance anxiety on ice."

She laughed, the sound echoing across the empty pond, startling a crow from a nearby pine. "I wasn't that good."

"You were that good. You made the hockey team look like toddlers." He gestured toward the bench near the warming hut. "Come on, Freeman. Show me if the city girl still remembers how."

They sat on the wooden bench that had been there since before either of them was born, their initials probably carved in it somewhere along with hundreds of others. Her skates were ancient rentals from the warming hut, a half-size too big and smelling faintly of mothballs and decades of other people's feet. His were the same scuffed hockey skates he'd worn at seventeen, the leather cracked and comfortable.

He laced his in practiced motions, then looked up to find her struggling with the complex crossing pattern of her laces. Without a word, he shifted closer and took over, his hands gentle and efficient as he threaded and pulled, adjusted and tied. The gesture was intimate in a way that had nothing to do with romance and everything to do with care.

"There." He gave the bow a final tug. "Not too tight?"

She flexed her ankle, testing. "Perfect."

He stood first, steady despite the blades, and offered both hands. "Come on, Freeman. Show me what you've got."

She took his hands and let him pull her onto the ice, her muscles remembering the motion even after years away. The first glide was tentative, finding her balance, but then muscle memory kicked in and she was moving, smooth and sure. The cold air bit at her cheeks, making them sting. Her breath came in visible puffs.

For ten perfect minutes there was no ex-husband, no broken furnaces, no secret growing beneath her sweater that would change everything. Just the scrape of blades on ice, the cold bite of winter air in her lungs, and Caleb's surprised laughter when she spun him in a circle until he nearly fell, his arms windmilling comically.

"Show-off," he accused, but he was grinning.

"You love it," she shot back without thinking.

The words hung between them for a heartbeat, loaded with meaning neither of them was ready to examine. Then Caleb pushed off, chasing her around the rink with the determined clumsiness of someone who'd never quite mastered grace on ice.

When they finally coasted to a stop near the warming hut, both breathing hard and grinning like idiots, he still hadn't let go of her hands. His fingers were warm through their gloves, his grip steady.

"Ellie." His voice was serious now, the playfulness draining away.

She looked up, snowflakes starting to fall again in fat, lazy drifts. One landed on his hat brim, another on his shoulder.

"I don't know what you're running from," he said quietly, carefully, like he was trying not to spook her. "But you're safe here. You and—" His gaze flicked down, just for a second, to where her coat hid the tiniest curve, then back to her eyes. "Whoever else you brought with you."

Her breath caught in her throat, all the air leaving her lungs at once.

He saw it. Of course he saw it. Saw everything.

"I'm not asking you to tell me," he added quickly. "Not before you're ready. Just wanted you to know. You're safe. You're wanted. And whatever you need—space, time, help, a warm place to land—you've got it. No strings. No expectations. Just... safety."

The ice creaked softly beneath them, settling under their weight. Somewhere in the trees that lined the pond, a branch dumped its load of snow with a muffled whump, the sound like a period at the end of a sentence.

Ellie felt the tears start before she could stop them, hot against her frozen cheeks. She hadn't cried like this in months—not since the day she'd sat in her lawyer's office signing papers that ended her marriage. Hadn't let herself cry because crying meant feeling, and feeling hurt too much.

But here, with Caleb's steady presence and the snow falling like absolution, she couldn't hold it back anymore.

He pulled her in without hesitation—not a hug, not quite, just close enough that she could rest her forehead against his coat and breathe in pine and woodsmoke and the indefinable scent that was just him. Close enough to feel safe. Close enough to fall apart without falling down.

"I've got you," he murmured into her hair, his voice barely above a whisper. "I've got you, Ellie. You're not alone."

And for the first time in months—maybe years—she believed someone actually did.

Chapter 7

Ellie cried for exactly thirty-seven seconds.

She counted them the way her therapist in Las Vegas had taught her during those first awful weeks after she'd left—breathe in for four, hold for four, out for four—until the storm passed and all that was left was the wet spot on Caleb's coat and the embarrassing hiccup she couldn't quite swallow.

He didn't move, didn't shush her, didn't offer empty platitudes. He simply held her steady on ice skates while snow collected on both their shoulders like a benediction, like the sky itself was trying to blanket them in quiet grace.

When she finally pulled back, swiping at her cheeks with mittens that were more dampness than wool now, he handed her a folded red bandanna from his pocket without comment.

"Sheriff standard issue," he said, his tone deliberately light. "Tears, blood, the occasional exploding pen. This one's clean. Mostly."

She laughed despite herself, a watery snort that made Tripod—who had insisted on coming and was now lying on the ice like a furry ottoman, apparently unbothered by the cold—thump his tail in approval.

Caleb's eyes were soft when she finally looked up at him. "Better?"

"Getting there." She blew her nose with as much dignity as she could muster, which wasn't much. "I'm sorry. Hormones are —"

She stopped dead, the words freezing on her tongue.

He waited, patient as winter.

She tried again, her heart hammering. "I'm pregnant."

The words hung between them, small and enormous all at once. Caleb's face didn't change—no shock, no recoil, no pity. Just a slow exhale that fogged white in the cold air, and something in his eyes that might have been relief.

"Figured," he said simply.

She blinked. "You... figured?"

"Ellie, I've been a single dad for five years. I know what morning sickness looks like, even when someone's trying to hide it. The way you turned green at the smell of bacon this morning? The dizzy spell? Plus—" he gestured vaguely at her middle "—you keep touching your stomach like you're making sure something's still there."

Heat flooded her face despite the cold. "I thought I was being subtle."

"You were. Most people wouldn't notice. But I'm trained to notice things." His mouth curved slightly. "And I pay attention when it matters."

The last part was said so quietly she almost missed it.

"Mark?" he asked after a moment, his voice carefully neutral.

She nodded once, her stomach knotting. "But he doesn't— he's not calling about the baby. He doesn't want anything to do with the baby."

Caleb waited, letting the silence stretch until she was ready to fill it.

"He's calling about money," she said finally, the words bitter on her tongue. "About the house we owned together, the one I bought mostly with my inheritance from my parents. About the settlement that he thinks isn't fair, even though he's the one who —"

She stopped, swallowed hard against the memories that threatened to surface. The bruise on her arm that she'd explained away as clumsiness. The hole in the bedroom wall from where he'd punched it during an argument. The way he'd grabbed her wrist hard enough to leave marks when she'd said she was keeping the baby, his face twisted with rage as he'd called her selfish, stupid, said she was ruining everything they'd built.

The threats that had started after she'd left. Not physical—he was too smart for that now, knew she could press charges. But financial threats. Legal threats. Promises that he'd make her life hell, that he'd take everything, that she'd regret making him look bad in front of his colleagues.

"He doesn't want the baby," she continued, forcing the words out. "He made that very clear. When I told him I was pregnant, he told me to 'take care of it' or he'd file for divorce. When I said I was keeping it, he said I was trapping him, that I was selfish, that children would ruin everything. He wanted me to sign papers saying he had no parental rights or responsibilities. His lawyer drew them up and everything."

Caleb's jaw tightened almost imperceptibly. "Did you sign them?"

"No. My lawyer advised against it. Said it could complicate things down the road, that he might change his mind and cause problems. That it's better to establish child support obligations now, even if he never pays them." She twisted the damp bandanna between her hands. "So now he's angry about that too. Angry that I won't just let him walk away clean. But he doesn't want custody or visitation or anything to do with the baby. He just wants—"

"Control," Caleb finished quietly. "Wants to make you pay for not doing what he wanted. For not being who he wanted you to be."

She looked up at him sharply. "How did you—"

"Seen it before. In my work." His eyes were dark, serious. "Guys who can't stand that they don't get to dictate the terms anymore. So they use whatever leverage they have—money, property, threats—to maintain power. Not because they actually care about the outcome. Just because they can't stand losing."

The accuracy of his assessment made her chest tight. "My lawyer filed a restraining order last month. Not because he'd done anything recent, but because she was worried. Said the pattern of behavior was escalating. The calls, the messages, showing up at my office. The judge granted a temporary order but said we'd need more evidence for a permanent one."

"And he's violating it by calling you." It wasn't a question.

"Different phone number. Probably a burner. He's careful. Always careful." She heard the bitterness in her own voice. "That's why I left Vegas. My lawyer said it might be good to have some distance while everything gets sorted out. Let him cool down, give the legal process time to work. I have until January to respond to his latest filing about the house."

Caleb was quiet for a long moment, his hand still holding hers though neither of them was skating anymore. "You should document those calls. Save the voicemails. My office can help if you need to file an updated order."

"I don't want to cause trouble—"

"Ellie." He waited until she looked at him. "Protecting yourself and your baby isn't causing trouble. It's being smart. And if he shows up here, if he comes to Estrella Ridge, I want to know. Immediately. You call me, doesn't matter what time, doesn't matter if you think it's not important enough. You call."

The fierce protectiveness in his voice made something in her chest crack wider.

"He's not... he never hit me," she said, needing him to understand. "Not really. Once he grabbed my arm hard enough to bruise, and another time he pushed me during an argument. But mostly it was just—"

"Just?" Caleb's voice was very quiet, very controlled. "Ellie, there's no 'just' with this stuff. Grabbing, pushing, punching walls, making you afraid—that's all violence. It doesn't have to leave visible marks to count."

She nodded, tears threatening again. She'd heard this from her therapist, from her lawyer, from the women at the domestic violence support group she'd attended twice before deciding she couldn't handle hearing everyone's stories while carrying her own.

But hearing it from Caleb, in his steady sheriff's voice that held no judgment—only concern and something fiercer—made it feel more real somehow.

"How far along?" he asked after a moment, shifting back to practical matters.

"Thirteen weeks tomorrow." She pressed a hand to her belly without thinking. "Doctor says everything looks perfect. Strong heartbeat. Good measurements. I have an ultrasound scheduled for next week, but obviously I'll need to reschedule that now."

"We can help with that. Doc Martinez in town is good—she's delivered half the babies in Estrella Ridge for the past twenty years. If you're staying a while, might be good to establish care here. Just in case."

The casual "we" made her heart do something complicated. Made it feel like she wasn't alone in this. Like her problems were problems someone else was willing to share.

Ellie choked on a laugh that was half sob. "You're not... freaked out? About all this? The ex-husband, the legal mess, the baby, the fact that I'm basically homeless and hiding out in your spare room?"

"Ellie, I spent two tours overseas watching miracles happen in places that should've only had funerals. I learned a long time ago that babies are never the problem. People who hurt the people carrying them—they're the problem. But babies?" He shook his head. "Babies are always the solution. Always hope. Always worth protecting."

A gust of wind rattled the warming hut, making the Christmas lights sway. Tripod stood up, shook himself with his peculiar three-legged balance, and promptly sat on Caleb's skate like he was claiming territory.

Caleb looked down at the dog, then at Ellie. "We should head back. Noah will be home soon, and Mabel's probably already called six people to report that my truck's been parked at Miller's Pond for forty-five minutes. By dinner she'll have us eloped to Vegas."

Ellie's laugh was watery but genuine. "Does she really have nothing better to do?"

"This is her better thing to do. The woman lives for this." He started skating backward, tugging her with him toward the bench. "But she's harmless. Mostly. And she makes a mean apple pie, so we tolerate the gossip."

They turned in their skates—Caleb's to the wooden cubby where he'd apparently been storing them for years, Ellie's back to the rental rack. Tripod trotted proudly ahead like he'd invented winter recreation, his gait lopsided but confident.

On the drive home, Caleb kept the radio low, some old Vince Gill Christmas song neither of them sang along to. But halfway back to town, he reached across the console and took her hand, threading their fingers together like it was the most natural thing in the world.

"You're safe here," he said again, his thumb tracing circles on her knuckles. "Whatever's coming, whatever he tries to pull— you're not facing it alone anymore. I meant what I said. No strings, no expectations. Just safety. For both of you."

She looked at their joined hands, at the way her smaller fingers fit between his larger ones, and felt something shift in her chest. Something that had been locked tight for so long she'd forgotten it could open.

When they pulled into his driveway, Noah burst out the front door before the truck even stopped, coat half-zipped, boots on the wrong feet, a huge grin splitting his face.

"Ellie! Guess what! Pastor Mike says we can borrow the church van to pick up the live nativity animals tomorrow, and he said you're in charge of marketing so you get to name the donkey! I made a list! Number one is Sir Neighs-a-Lot, but number two is Donkey Hotey, which Mrs. Mabel says is 'cultured' but I don't know what that means!"

Caleb raised an eyebrow at her in the rearview mirror, amusement dancing in his eyes.

Ellie sighed dramatically, but she was smiling. "I've always wanted to name a donkey."

Noah grabbed her hand the second she stepped out of the truck, his grip sticky with what was probably fruit snacks. "Come see! I made you a whole presentation with pictures I printed from the library computer! Daddy, can Ellie stay for dinner? Please? I'm making my famous spaghetti!"

"Your famous spaghetti is Ragu from a jar," Caleb pointed

out.

"But I add the secret ingredient!"

"Italian seasoning is not a secret, bud. It's literally labeled 'Italian seasoning.'"

"But the *amount* is secret! That's what makes it famous!"

Caleb followed them inside, shaking his head, but Ellie caught the look on his face—something dangerously close to contentment. To peace. To a man who'd been missing something for a long time and was only just realizing he might have found it.

Later, after Noah was asleep and the house was quiet except for the crackle of the fireplace, Ellie stood at the kitchen sink washing the last of the spaghetti bowls. Caleb came up behind her, reached around to take the bowl from her hands.

"I can do dishes," she protested weakly.

"You did bedtime story, three rounds of Go Fish, and convinced Noah that no, we cannot have a donkey as a house pet even if it's really, really small. You're off duty."

He dried the bowl, set it in the cabinet with careful precision, then leaned back against the counter, arms crossed. In the soft light from the pendant lamp above the sink, he looked younger somehow. Less sheriff, more just a man in his own kitchen at the end of a long day.

"Tomorrow's Saturday," he said. "Town tree-lighting's at six. Noah's been asking if you'll come. No pressure," he added quickly. "I know it's a lot, the whole town and the questions and Mabel making a spectacle. But if you want to come, we'd... I'd like you to be there."

Ellie's stomach flipped. The whole town. Gossip. Questions. Mark's calls still burning a hole in her phone, the threat of him showing up, of everything crashing down around her.

She opened her mouth to make an excuse, to say she wasn't ready.

Caleb spoke first, reading her hesitation. "You don't owe anyone explanations, Ellie. Not about why you're here, not about what you're running from, not about anything. But if you want to hide out here with hot chocolate and old John Wayne movies, that's fine too. Whatever you need. No pressure."

She studied his face—steady, kind, unfairly handsome in the soft light. The face of a man who meant what he said, who offered safety without demanding anything in return.

"I'll come," she said. "But only if you promise to protect me from Mabel's matchmaking."

His grin was slow and devastating, transforming his whole face. "No promises. Woman's sneakier than a coyote in a henhouse. But I'll do my best."

He pushed off the counter, paused just long enough that she thought—hoped?—he might touch her again, might pull her close the way he had on the ice. Then he simply brushed a knuckle across her cheek, feather-light, there and gone.

"Night, Ellie."

"Night, Caleb."

She listened to his footsteps on the stairs, the creak of floorboards overhead, the soft click of his bedroom door. Then she placed both hands on her belly, feeling the tiny life flutter inside like a butterfly testing its wings.

"We're okay, little one," she whispered into the quiet. "I think we might actually be okay. He doesn't want you—your biological father doesn't want you—but that doesn't mean you're not wanted. That doesn't mean you're not loved. Because I want you. And Caleb... I think maybe Caleb wants us too."

The baby gave a strong kick in response, as if to say *I know. I'm not worried. Are you?* And Ellie realized with startling clarity that for the first time in months, she wasn't worried. Not about this, anyway. Not about whether she'd made the right choice keeping this baby. Not about whether she could do this alone.

Because she wasn't alone. Not anymore.

Outside, the snow kept falling, covering every old track, making the whole world new. Erasing the roads that led away, as if the universe itself was conspiring to keep her here.

And maybe—just maybe—that wasn't such a bad thing after all.

Chapter 8

Saturday arrived wrapped in sunshine so bright it hurt.

Ellie stood at the bedroom window watching Noah and Tripod chase each other through the front yard, leaving crooked tracks in the fresh snow that sparkled like crushed diamonds. The sky was that impossible shade of blue that only happened in Colorado winters—so vivid it looked painted on, so clear you could see every detail of the mountains in the distance.

Noah fell backward into a drift, arms and legs spread wide to make a snow angel. Tripod immediately pounced on him, the dog's enthusiastic licking making Noah's shrieks of laughter carry all the way to the second floor.

Caleb was out there too, pushing the snowblower down the sidewalk with the same calm focus he brought to everything. He'd been at it since before sunrise—she'd heard the engine roar to life while it was still dark, had watched from her window as he'd cleared not just his own walk but Mabel's next door, and the Martinez house across the street where Carol Jean's husband was recovering from knee surgery.

Every few passes he glanced up at her window. When their eyes met for the third time, he lifted a gloved hand in a small wave that did stupid things to her pulse.

She waved back, then immediately felt sixteen again—giddy and awkward and completely out of her depth.

Downstairs smelled like cinnamon rolls and impending cardiac arrest. Caleb's once-a-year Christmas carb binge, he'd told her last night, a tradition that started when Noah was two and Sarah had declared that December weekends required "foods that make your arteries cry but your soul sing."

Noah had already eaten two rolls by the time Ellie made it to the kitchen, and was lobbying hard for a third while Caleb pretended to negotiate.

"Two and a half," Noah countered, holding up sticky fingers as evidence of his mathematical reasoning.

"Two and a quarter," Caleb said with the solemnity of someone negotiating a hostage situation.

"Deal!" Noah licked icing off his thumb, then noticed Ellie in the doorway. "Ellie! Daddy said you get the first fresh one today because you're growing a tiny human and tiny humans like frosting. He said it's science."

Ellie froze halfway down the stairs, her hand gripping the railing. Caleb's eyes flicked to hers—apology and amusement warring for space in his expression.

"I may have mentioned it," he said under his breath, turning back to the pan of rolls with studied casualness.

Noah looked between them, confused by their reactions. "Did I say the secret wrong? Daddy said it wasn't a secret anymore now that you told him. He said secrets are only secrets if they're meant to be kept, but good news should be shared with people who matter."

Ellie's throat tightened. She descended the last few steps slowly, then crouched to Noah's height, bringing herself eye-level with him. "You said it perfectly, Noah. And you're absolutely right—it's not a secret. I am growing a tiny human. A baby."

Noah's face lit up like the town square at dusk, pure joy radiating from every pore. "Is it a boy or a girl?"

"We don't know yet. Won't know for a few more weeks."

"Can it be a boy? I already know how boys work. Girls are probably different. Jake Hensley says his baby sister cries all the time and smells like sour milk."

Caleb choked on his coffee, coughing hard into his fist.

Ellie laughed so hard her eyes watered, the sound bursting out of her with a force that surprised them both. "We'll put in a request, but I can't make any promises. Babies have a way of being whoever they're meant to be."

"That's okay. If it's a girl, I can learn. Mrs. Patterson says learning new things builds character." Noah leaned in conspiratorially, his voice dropping to a stage whisper. "Is the baby's daddy coming to visit? 'Cause if he is, I can share my room. We have bunk beds. Well, we don't *have* bunk beds, but Daddy could probably build them. He's really good at building stuff."

The innocent question landed like a punch to the sternum. Ellie felt her smile freeze, felt Caleb's attention sharpen even though he kept his back to them, ostensibly focused on transferring cinnamon rolls to a plate.

"No, honey. The baby's daddy won't be visiting. He's... he's not going to be part of my or the baby's lives."

Noah processed this with the serious consideration of someone trying to understand adult complications. "Like how some kids at school have daddies who live far away? Or like how my mommy's in heaven?"

"More like the first one," Ellie said carefully. "He lives far away and he's made a choice not to be involved. But that's okay, because this baby is going to have lots of people who love them anyway."

"Like you," Noah said with certainty. "And me. And Daddy. And Tripod. And Mrs. Mabel, even though she's kinda scary sometimes. And Pastor Mike. And—"

"That's a lot of people," Ellie interrupted gently, her voice thick. "That's more than enough."

Noah seemed satisfied with this. He returned to his cinnamon roll with the focus of someone who'd solved a complex problem and could now move on to more important matters—like whether chocolate milk was an appropriate breakfast beverage.

Caleb finally turned around, sliding a plate across the counter to Ellie. The cinnamon roll was enormous, dripping with cream cheese frosting, still steaming slightly. "Eat. Doctor's orders."

"You're not a doctor."

"Sheriff's orders, then. Same authority, better uniform." His smile was soft, meant just for her. "And Noah's right—tiny humans need frosting. Also protein, but we'll get to that after you've had sugar."

By five-thirty they were bundled into every layer they owned and walking the three blocks to the town square. Noah rode on Caleb's shoulders, narrating every Christmas light like a tour guide who'd memorized the script. Tripod trotted alongside on his festive red leash, wearing felt reindeer antlers that listed dangerously to the left, giving him a perpetually quizzical expression.

The square was already packed when they arrived. Booths sold hot cocoa and kettle corn, the sweet and salty smells mingling in the cold air. The high school brass band played "Carol of the Bells" with more enthusiasm than accuracy, the trumpets slightly sharp and the trombones dragging behind. Children darted between adult legs like minnows through a reef, their laughter high and bright.

White lights had been strung everywhere—wrapped around every tree trunk, draped between lampposts, outlining the gazebo where the town council held summer concerts. The Christmas tree itself stood in the center of the square, a massive blue spruce that had to be thirty feet tall, not yet lit but already majestic in the fading daylight.

Mabel Hensley stood on a hay bale near the gazebo, directing traffic with a candy cane the size of a baseball bat, her voice carrying over the crowd. She wore a different sweater today—this one featuring a three-dimensional Santa face with a beard made of actual cotton balls.

She spotted them immediately, her eyes locking onto Ellie with laser precision.

"Ellie Freeman! Front and center! We need you for the countdown!"

Ellie tried to shrink behind Caleb's broad back, which was pointless because he was moving forward, not backward, and she was essentially using him as a very ineffective human shield.

Mabel seized her arm with surprising strength for a woman in her seventies. "You're co-chair of the festival committee. Co-chairs stand on the bandstand and look official during the tree lighting. It's tradition."

"I'm not dressed for official," Ellie hissed, gesturing at her jeans and Caleb's borrowed parka that was three sizes too big. "I look like I'm wearing a tent."

"Nonsense." Mabel propelled her forward through the crowd with the unstoppable force of a woman on a mission. "Caleb, bring that handsome sheriff self up here too. We need muscle in case the star gets stuck again like last year."

"The star weighs four pounds," Caleb muttered, but he followed with the resigned air of a man who'd lost this battle years ago and knew better than to fight it again.

The bandstand was actually just a raised platform with steps on three sides, built decades ago for the town band and never updated. It was decorated now with garland and red bows, and standing on it gave Ellie a clear view of what had to be two hundred faces staring up at her.

Two hundred familiar faces, some she recognized from childhood, others new. All watching with the unabashed curiosity of small-town residents who'd heard the gossip and wanted to see the drama firsthand.

Pastor Mike waved from the front row, his kind face creased in a welcoming smile. The diner owner, Tom Henderson, stood nearby holding a toddler on his shoulders. Half the women from the casserole brigade clustered together, clutching phones for pictures. Mrs. Patterson had her camera out, the flash already blinding people.

Someone started chanting "Speech! Speech!" and others picked it up until it became a roar.

Ellie's stomach lurched. Her hands went clammy inside her gloves. The faces below started to blur together, too many eyes, too much attention, too much expectation.

This was a mistake. She shouldn't have come. Should have stayed hidden in Caleb's house where it was safe, where she could pretend the rest of the world didn't exist.

Caleb stepped up beside her, close enough that their shoulders touched. His hand found the small of her back, warm and steady even through her thick coat. He leaned in, his breath ghosting across her ear.

"Breathe," he murmured so quietly only she could hear. "They're not here to judge. They're here because they're happy you're home. This town loved Ruth, and they love everyone Ruth loved. You're family to them, even if you've been gone. Just breathe. I've got you."

Pastor Mike appeared on the platform, climbing the steps with the careful attention of someone whose knees weren't what they used to be. He handed Ellie a microphone like it was a live grenade, his smile encouraging.

She stared at the microphone, at the expectant faces, at the lights and the tree and the sheer overwhelming *muchness* of it all.

Two hundred people waiting.

Her mouth opened. Nothing came out.

Then Noah's small voice piped up from where Caleb had set him down in the front row, clear as a bell in the sudden quiet. "Tell them about the donkey names! And how you're having a baby! And how Tripod picked you!"

Laughter rippled through the crowd, warm and genuine. The tension broke like ice under spring sun.

Ellie found herself laughing too, the sound surprising her. She clicked the mic on, and feedback squealed for a second before someone adjusted something.

"Hi, everybody." Her voice echoed across the square, amplified and strange to her own ears. "I wasn't planning on public speaking tonight. Or any night, really. But Noah's right— we do still need a name for the nativity donkey. Current front-runner is Sir Neighs-a-Lot, but I'm accepting bribes in the form of Christmas cookies."

Cheers erupted. Someone shouted, "I vote for Donkey Oatie!"

Another voice: "Burrito Supreme!"

A third: "Judge Judy! Because she has opinions!"

The suggestions got progressively more ridiculous, and Ellie felt herself relaxing into the absurdity of it all. These weren't strangers. These were people who'd known her grandmother, who'd watched her grow up, who remembered her as the shy girl who'd left for college and never looked back. Until now.

"Voting closes at the live nativity on Christmas Eve," she announced when the suggestions finally died down. "Until then, thank you for welcoming me back to Estrella Ridge. It's been—" her voice caught unexpectedly "—it's good to be home. Even if I'm only here temporarily. Even if my furnace is frozen and my car is in the shop. Your casseroles alone have made it worth it."

More laughter, this time accompanied by knowing looks and elbow nudges.

"And yes," she added, deciding to just rip the bandaid off, "I am having a baby. Due in June. No, before you ask, there's no father in the picture. His choice, not mine. No, I don't need anyone to fix that situation. Yes, I know what caused it." That got a huge laugh. "But I would appreciate any and all advice about babies, because I have approximately zero experience and I'm terrified."

The crowd erupted in applause and shouts of "You'll do great!" and "Call me anytime!" and "I have three boxes of baby clothes in my attic!"

Ellie handed the microphone to Caleb like it was burning her hand.

He took it without hesitation, his presence solid and calm beside her. "On behalf of the sheriff's department, I'd like to remind everyone that mistletoe does not grant legal immunity." Pause for laughter. "Also, the tree's been inspected, the star is secure, and if anyone tries to climb it again like Tommy Martinez did last year, you're spending Christmas in a cell decorating it with paper chains. Don't test me."

He handed the mic back to Pastor Mike, who led a quick prayer—short, heartfelt, and mercifully free of any references to Ellie's reproductive status.

Then the countdown began.

Ten.

Nine.

Eight...

Caleb's hand found hers in the growing darkness, fingers threading together with the ease of practice, like they'd been holding hands for years instead of days.

Three.

Two.

One.

The tree exploded into brilliance—thousands of white lights reflecting off snow and eyes and hearts. The effect was stunning, almost magical, like the tree itself had become a conduit for starlight. The band struck up "O Christmas Tree" with gusto. Children shrieked in delight. Adults applauded.

Noah launched himself at Ellie's legs from the front row with the force of a small missile. She scooped him up automatically, staggering slightly under his weight. He smelled like hot chocolate and candy canes and little boy, his arms wrapping around her neck with absolute trust.

Caleb's arm slid around her waist, steadying them both, his hand splaying wide across her hip. For one long moment the three of them stood wrapped together on that platform—four, if you counted the tiny heartbeat under her coat—surrounded by colored light and woodsmoke and the sound of people singing slightly off-key.

Ellie felt something crack open inside her chest, something that had been frozen solid since the day Mark had shoved her against the kitchen counter and told her she was ruining his life. Since the day she'd packed her car in the middle of the night while he was at work, leaving behind everything that wouldn't fit.

Caleb leaned close, his lips near her ear so his words wouldn't carry. "You okay?"

She turned just enough that her cheek brushed his, felt the rasp of stubble and the warmth of his breath. "I really am."

Above them, the star glowed steady and bright, refusing to lean or falter.

And for the first time in a very long time, Ellie Freeman

believed in miracles again. Not the big, flashy kind that split seas or raised the dead. But the small, quiet kind that showed up in snowstorms and held your hand in the dark and made sure you knew you weren't alone. Those kinds of miracles, she was learning, were more than enough.

Chapter 9

The night didn't end with the tree lighting.

After the crowd thinned and the cocoa ran out, Mabel declared an "emergency festival planning session" at Henderson's Diner. Translation: everyone who mattered—and half who only thought they did—crammed into red vinyl booths to argue about donkey names and whether the live nativity needed theatrical lighting or if that was "too Broadway" for Estrella Ridge.

Ellie tried to beg off, exhaustion pulling at her bones like an undertow. But Noah had already fallen asleep against her shoulder on the walk from the square, his dead weight warm and trusting, drooling slightly on her borrowed coat. When she tried to shift him to Caleb, Noah's arms tightened around her neck in his sleep, refusing to let go.

Caleb simply adjusted the boy's weight more securely in her arms and said, "We're in for one coffee. Then home. I promise."

One coffee turned into two pieces of pecan pie that Tom Henderson insisted were "on the house for the festival co-chair." It turned into a spirited debate over whether the wise men should arrive on ATVs or camels, with Carol Jean Martinez advocating passionately for "authenticity" while half the room pointed out that insurance for camels was astronomical and someone would definitely get spit on.

"The youth group could ride the ATVs," suggested Jake Hensley's mother. "Put some tinsel on the handlebars, call it good."

"That's not biblical," Mrs. Patterson protested.

"Neither are ATVs, Margaret, but here we are in the twenty-first century."

Ellie sat tucked against Caleb's side in the corner booth, Noah's head now in her lap, his small body radiating heat like a furnace. Tripod snored under the table, occasionally kicking in his sleep and bumping her shin. Every time she tried to shift to get more comfortable, Caleb's arm tightened fractionally across her shoulders—not restrictive, just present. A quiet reminder that she could lean if she needed to.

Across the table, Mabel watched them with the satisfaction of a cat who'd not only caught the canary but had gotten it to sing show tunes.

The debate raged on. Carol Jean wanted fog machines for "atmospheric effect." Pastor Mike worried about smoke alarms. Someone suggested using dry ice, which sparked an entirely new argument about whether that was safe around livestock.

At 10:17 p.m., Caleb stood abruptly, ending all discussion with the authority of a man who'd decided enough was enough. "We're done. Donkey's name is getting decided by the kids at Sunday school tomorrow. ATVs with tinsel. No fog machines— the volunteer fire department said no last year and I'm not overruling them. Meeting adjourned."

Mabel opened her mouth to protest, her expression indignant.

Caleb stared her down with the flat, professional gaze that probably worked wonders on drunk drivers and teenagers caught shoplifting. "Mabel. It's past ten. Some of us have kids who need to be in bed. Meeting. Adjourned."

Mabel's mouth snapped shut with an audible click. She looked like she wanted to argue but recognized the losing battle when she saw it.

Outside, the temperature had dropped hard, the kind of cold that made your nose hairs freeze and your lungs hurt. Their breath hung in clouds that looked solid enough to grab. Caleb settled Noah higher against his chest—the boy had transferred to his father without waking—and offered Ellie his free arm.

She took it without thinking, grateful for the stability as they navigated icy sidewalks that hadn't been salted yet.

They walked the quiet blocks home under streetlamps draped in icicle lights that swayed slightly in the wind. Snow crunched under their boots, the sound loud in the stillness.

Tripod's enthusiastic sniffing of every snowbank and fire hydrant provided a soundtrack of investigation.

Halfway home, Ellie spoke, her voice low so she wouldn't wake Noah. "You didn't have to rescue me from Mabel. I could have handled it."

"Yeah, you could have." He didn't look at her, his focus on navigating the sidewalk's uneven patches. "But Mabel was two minutes from asking about wedding colors. That qualified as an emergency rescue situation."

Ellie snorted softly. "She already texted me a Pinterest board. It's called 'Rustic Winter Sheriff Chic.' There are at least forty pins."

Caleb groaned, a sound of pure suffering. "I'm confiscating her phone."

"Good luck with that. I think it's surgically attached."

"I'll get a warrant."

They reached the house, the porch light glowing warm and welcoming. Inside, the fireplace had burned down to embers, the Christmas tree lights the only other illumination. The house smelled like pine and the lingering sweetness of cinnamon rolls.

Caleb carried Noah straight upstairs without turning on additional lights, his feet knowing the path by heart. Ellie banked the fire, added two logs from the basket, and started hot water for tea she wasn't entirely sure she wanted. Her body was exhausted but her mind was wired, buzzing with the energy of too many people, too much attention, too many feelings she wasn't ready to examine.

When Caleb came back down, he'd changed from his uniform into sweatpants and an ancient Army Rangers t-shirt that clung in ways that should probably be illegal. His hair was slightly mussed from pulling off his shirt, and he hadn't bothered with socks. His bare feet on the hardwood made almost no sound.

He leaned in the kitchen doorway, watching her measure chamomile like it was a precise science experiment requiring her full concentration.

"You don't have to mother-hen me," she said without turning around, hyperaware of his gaze on her back.

"Noted." He crossed the kitchen in three long strides, took the tin of tea from her hand with gentle insistence, and set it aside. "Sit."

She sat at the table, too tired to argue.

He poured two mugs, added honey to hers the way she'd taken it in high school—another detail he'd remembered across twelve years and a lifetime of changes. He slid one mug across the table, then took the chair beside her instead of across from her. Close enough that she could feel the heat radiating from his body, smell the clean scent of his soap.

Silence stretched between them, comfortable but humming with unspoken things.

Finally he spoke, his voice quiet in the dim kitchen. "You asked me once, senior year, why I never came to church after my mom died."

Ellie went still, her hands wrapped around her mug. She remembered. Study hall, February, rain instead of snow. She'd invited him to youth group; he'd shut down so completely she'd never asked again. She had spent the rest of that year wondering what she'd said wrong, how she'd overstepped.

"I figured you'd forgotten," he said, staring into his tea.

"I don't forget much about you," she admitted before her brain could stop her mouth. The words hung in the air between them, too honest, too revealing.

His eyes flicked to hers, held. Something passed between them—recognition, maybe, or acknowledgment of the thing they'd been dancing around since she'd crashed back into his life.

"I was angry," he continued, his voice rough with memory. "At God, at cancer, at the universe. Didn't see the point in singing about joy to the world when everything felt broken. When watching your mom waste away to nothing felt like proof that either God didn't exist or He didn't care. Easier to just... not go. Not pretend."

He turned the mug in slow circles on the table, watching the liquid swirl. "Then Sarah died. One minute I had a wife and Noah had a mother. Next minute I'm a widower at twenty-six with a three-year-old who doesn't understand why Mommy won't wake up."

Ellie's throat tightened. She wanted to reach for his hand but wasn't sure if touch would be welcome or intrusive.

"I got really good at being angry after that," Caleb said. "Angry at every drunk driver I pulled over. Angry at God for taking two of the best people I knew. Angry at Sarah for leaving, even though that wasn't fair. Angry at myself for not being enough to make her stay, like I could have somehow prevented the illness."

He took a breath, let it out slowly. "Pastor Mike came by every week for a year. Just sat with me. Didn't preach, didn't push. Sometimes we talked. Sometimes we just sat in silence. He told me once that anger is just grief's bodyguard—that it stands in front of the pain and says 'you can't come in yet.'"

"Did it work?" Ellie asked softly. "Did you eventually let it in?"

"Not all at once. Little pieces at a time. Noah helped—he was so young, so innocent. His questions forced me to figure out what I actually believed versus what I was just angry about. He'd ask things like 'Is Mommy happy in heaven?' and I had to decide —did I believe she was somewhere good, or did I think death was just... nothing?"

"What did you decide?"

"That I wanted Noah to have hope. That even if I wasn't sure what I believed, I wanted him to believe his mom was somewhere beautiful. That love doesn't end just because someone stops breathing." He paused, then added quietly, "And somewhere along the way, I started believing it too. Not because someone convinced me, but because watching Noah heal, watching him still love and trust and hope—that felt like proof of something. Something bigger than random chance and bad luck."

The kitchen clock ticked. Outside, wind rattled the windows, but inside it was warm, safe, insulated from the cold.

"Tonight," Caleb continued, his voice rough, "watching you up there on that bandstand, scared half to death but still making people laugh, still being honest about being terrified—something shifted. You stood in front of this whole town and said 'I'm pregnant, I'm alone, I'm scared, and I need help.' That takes more courage than most people have."

He finally looked at her directly, his eyes intense in the dim light. "I don't know what all this means yet, Ellie. I don't know what God's doing or why you crashed your car on my stretch of highway. But I know I'm tired of being angry. Tired of playing it safe. Tired of pretending that having you here doesn't feel like —"

He stopped, seemed to reconsider his words.

"Like what?" she prompted, her heart hammering.

"Like coming home," he finished quietly. "I'm thirty-one years old, I've been a widower for five years, and I thought that part of my life was done. That I'd had my chance at love and lost it. That the best I could hope for was being a good dad and a decent sheriff and maybe not dying alone."

He reached across the small distance between them, covered her hand with his where it rested on the table. His palm was warm and calloused, his fingers gentle.

"Then you show up in a ditch, pregnant and running from a man who hurt you, and suddenly I'm feeling things I thought I'd buried with Sarah. Not the same things—" he added quickly. ""Not the same things," he added quickly. "What I had with Sarah wasn't my first love. That was you."

He let out a slow breath, like the truth still surprised him even after all these years. "You were the first person I ever loved enough to let go. I could see it—even back then. You were restless. Bigger than this place, or at least you thought you were. And loving you meant not asking you to stay somewhere that made you feel small."

His jaw tightened briefly, old hurt surfacing and passing just as quickly. "Losing you hurt. For a long time. Then I met Sarah, and the hurt stopped hurting so much. What we had was real—steady, chosen, built day by day. I loved her completely. I always will."

His gaze held Ellie's, open and unflinching. "Turns out the heart isn't a one-room house. It can hold more than one true love without betraying either of them. But…"

"But?" Ellie whispered.

"But what I'm feeling now—what I'm feeling for you—it's different. It's…" He struggled for words, his thumb tracing circles on her knuckles. "It's like I spent five years in black and white, just going through the motions. And suddenly there's color again. Suddenly I'm awake. And it's terrifying and wonderful and I have no idea what to do with it."

Ellie's breath caught in her chest, her pulse pounding so loud she was sure he could hear it.

"I'm a mess, Caleb," she said, needing him to understand. "I'm three months pregnant with another man's baby. A man who's probably going to make my life hell for the foreseeable future. I have no job, no home, legal bills I can't afford. I'm broken and scared and I don't have anything to offer you except —"

"Except you," he interrupted, his voice fierce. "You think I care about the rest of it? You think I look at you and see problems? I look at you and see strength. I see someone who left an abusive situation, who's protecting her child, who's brave enough to start over even when it's terrifying."

He shifted closer, his free hand coming up to cup her face, thumb brushing away a tear she hadn't realized had fallen. "I look at you and see the girl who tutored me in algebra even though I was probably hopeless. Who smiled at me in the hallway when most people didn't notice I existed. Who left for bigger things because she deserved bigger things. And I see the woman who came back—who's here, who's real, who's let me and Noah into her life even though she had every reason to keep us at arm's length."

"Caleb—"

"I'm not asking for anything you're not ready to give," he said against her forehead, his breath warm on her skin. "I'm not asking for promises or commitments or anything beyond right now. I'm just saying—don't run. Don't leave yet. Give this—give us—a real chance. Let me be here for you. Let Noah love you the way he's already decided to. Let yourself have a safe place to land while you figure out what comes next."

She closed her eyes, tears streaming freely now. "What if I hurt you? What if this all falls apart and Noah gets attached and I—"

"Then we'll deal with it," he said simply. "But I'd rather risk hurt than miss this. Miss you. I never forgot you, Ellie—not even when I was building a life with someone else. I loved my wife. Truly. But loving her didn't erase what you were to me. It just taught me that the heart can be faithful and still remember."

They sat like that for a long moment—his forehead pressed to hers, their breath mingling in the small space between them, his hands gentle on her face and her hand.

Then Ellie closed the distance and kissed him.

It was soft, tentative, tasting of salt from her tears and honey from the tea. His lips were warm and patient, moving against hers with careful reverence like she was something precious that might break.

When they pulled apart, she was crying harder, but she was also smiling.

"I don't know what I'm doing," she whispered.

"Me neither." His answering smile was crooked, vulnerable. "But I'm willing to figure it out if you are."

"Okay," she breathed. "Okay. I'll stay. Not just until my car's fixed. I'll stay and see where this goes. I'll stay and let myself hope that maybe—maybe this is exactly where I'm supposed to be."

He kissed her again, deeper this time, his hands sliding into her hair. She felt herself melting into him, all the walls she'd built crumbling like snow in spring.

When they finally broke apart, both breathing hard, he rested his forehead against hers again.

"Welcome home, Ellie Freeman," he murmured. "For real this time."

And sitting in that warm kitchen, wrapped in Caleb Brennan's arms with his son sleeping upstairs and her baby safe beneath her heart, Ellie finally—finally—felt like she'd found her way home.

Not to a place, but to a person.

Not to the past, but to a future she was brave enough to reach for.

Outside, the snow kept falling, soft and steady, covering every old track and making everything new again.

Inside, two broken people held each other and dared to believe that maybe—just maybe—broken pieces could make something beautiful when fitted together the right way.

And somewhere above them, whether it was the stars or heaven or just the quiet presence of grace, something settled into place like the final piece of a puzzle sliding home.

This, it seemed to say. *This is what you've been waiting for.*

And for the first time in longer than she could remember, Ellie Freeman believed it was true and she whispered a silent prayer of thanks.

Chapter 10

Sunday morning arrived with church bells and the smell of mild panic.

Ellie stood in front of the guest room mirror wearing the only dress she'd packed—a simple navy wrap that had fit perfectly at ten weeks and now strained heroically across her chest and hips. The bump was no longer deniable, no longer something she could hide with careful layering and strategic poses. She looked exactly like a woman who had secrets that were now public knowledge, cinnamon rolls for breakfast, and a sheriff downstairs making pancakes while humming "Joy to the World" slightly off-key.

She turned sideways, assessing. The dress still worked, technically. It covered everything that needed covering. But there was no mistaking the curve of her belly now, the way the fabric clung and revealed what had been easy to hide just days ago.

A soft knock at the doorframe. Caleb's voice, low and careful. "Ellie? Noah wants to know if you're ready for the reindeer pancake parade. Which apparently is different from regular pancakes and requires a witness."

"Two minutes," she called back, voice cracking slightly on the second word.

She heard him hesitate outside the door, heard the creak of floorboards as he shifted his weight. "Ellie? You don't have to come to church. Nobody's keeping attendance. If you're not ready for the full town spectacle two days in a row—"

"I want to come." She yanked a cardigan over the dress, buttoned it strategically over the most obvious curves, and opened the door before she could second-guess herself.

Caleb's gaze flicked over her once—quick, appreciative, carefully professional, then back to her face where it stayed with focused intensity. He was wearing a charcoal button-down that made his eyes look more gray than green, sleeves rolled to his forearms in a way that should not be as attractive as it was. Noah stood beside him in a clip-on tie featuring cartoon nativity animals and light-up Christmas tree sneakers that blinked red and green with every step.

"You look pretty," Noah announced with the blunt honesty of an eight-year-old. "Like the angel on our tree, only with better shoes and a baby in your tummy that we can actually see now."

Ellie felt heat flood her face despite her best efforts. "Thank you, sir. You look very handsome too."

Noah beamed, adjusting his tie with exaggerated care. "Daddy said I had to wear church clothes and not my dinosaur shirt because Jesus appreciates effort even if He doesn't care about fashion."

Caleb pinched the bridge of his nose. "That's... not exactly what I said."

"You said Jesus cares more about hearts than clothes, which means He doesn't care about fashion. Same thing."

"Not quite, but we're going with it." Caleb offered Ellie his arm like they were attending a ball instead of walking four blocks to church. "Shall we?"

The walk to Estrella Ridge Community Church was shorter than Ellie remembered, or maybe it just felt that way with Caleb's solid presence beside her and Noah skipping ahead, his shoes blinking like a mobile disco with every bounce. Half the town waved from porches, some calling out greetings, others just watching with the frank curiosity of people who'd heard all the gossip and wanted visual confirmation.

Mabel was stationed on the church steps like a festive bouncer, clipboard in hand, wearing a hat that appeared to be an entire nativity scene perched precariously on her gray curls.

"Front row's saved," she announced as they approached, her tone brooking no argument. "I threatened Mrs. Jorgensen with my fruitcake recipe if she tried to claim it. She moved to the third row without complaint."

"Mabel, we don't need—" Caleb started.

"Front row," Mabel repeated, her eyes sharp despite the cheerful smile. "You three are family, and family sits up front where we can see them. Besides, half the congregation is here to stare anyway. Might as well give them a good view and get it over with."

Ellie wanted to argue, wanted to hide in the back where she could slip out unnoticed if everything became too much. But Mabel was already ushering them through the heavy wooden doors with the determination of a sheepdog herding particularly stubborn sheep.

Inside, the sanctuary smelled like pine and candle wax and decades of coffee hours. The ceiling was vaulted, exposed beams dark with age. Stained glass windows caught the morning sun, throwing colored light across the wooden pews—ruby reds and sapphire blues and emerald greens that made everything feel like being inside a kaleidoscope.

The sanctuary was already three-quarters full. Heads swiveled as they entered, tracking their progress down the center aisle. Whispers followed them like ducklings, not quite subtle enough to be discreet.

"Is that really her?"

"I heard she's staying at his place."

"Three months along, Mabel said."

"They look good together, don't they?"

Caleb's hand found the small of Ellie's back as they walked, a steady pressure that said *I'm right here, you're not alone, keep walking.* Noah skipped ahead to their pew—front row, left side, exactly where Mabel had promised—and climbed in without any of the reverence most children reserved for church.

Ellie slid into the pew, grateful for the cushioned seat. Caleb followed, settling close enough that their thighs touched. Noah immediately climbed into Ellie's lap without asking permission, settling like he belonged there, his small weight warm and trusting.

The organ wheezed to life, playing the opening notes of "O Come, All Ye Faithful" with more enthusiasm than skill. The congregation rose, hymnals rustling, voices joining in that peculiar community chorus where nobody was quite on the same note but everyone meant it sincerely.

Ellie opened her mouth to sing and found her throat too tight, her eyes burning with unexpected tears. Caleb's hand found hers in the hymnal they were sharing, their fingers tangling around the worn pages.

Pastor Mike took the pulpit after the hymn, his kind face creased in a smile that reached his eyes. He was probably sixty, with silver hair and the sort of gentle authority that came from decades of loving difficult people through hard times.

"Good morning, church. I see some familiar faces have come home for Christmas."

His eyes landed on Ellie, warm and welcoming, and she felt her face heat. But there was no judgment in his gaze, no condemnation. Just genuine gladness.

"We're going to talk this morning about prodigals," he continued, opening his Bible with practiced ease. "But not the way you might expect. Luke 15—everyone knows it. Rebellious son, distant country, pig slop, the father running down the road with his robe hiked up like a madman."

Gentle laughter rippled through the congregation.

"But here's what I want you to notice," Pastor Mike said, leaning forward slightly. "The father doesn't wait for the son to clean up first. Doesn't make him prove he's changed. Doesn't require a resume of good behavior before throwing the party. He runs—*runs*, which no respectable middle-eastern patriarch would ever do—while the son is still far off. Still filthy. Still reeking of pigs and bad choices."

Ellie tried to focus on the stained-glass windows instead of the sermon, but Pastor Mike's voice was impossible to ignore.

"Grace isn't earned by perfect attendance or perfect choices," he continued, his voice gentle but firm. "It's lavished on the ones brave enough to walk back through the door. It's given to the ones who show up broken and scared and honest about their mess. The father in this story doesn't love the son because he came home. He loved him the whole time he was gone. Coming home just meant the son finally let himself receive what was always already his."

When the service ended and the receiving line formed—because apparently that was a thing at Estrella Ridge Community Church—Caleb kept one hand on Ellie's waist and the other on Noah's shoulder, a quiet shield against the well-meaning onslaught.

People hugged her, welcomed her back, asked zero direct questions about the obvious curve under her cardigan while somehow managing to convey that they knew, they understood, and they were happy she was here. Estrella Ridge manners at their finest—all the awareness, none of the nosiness. At least not to her face.

"So glad you're back, honey."

"You look wonderful."

"That baby's lucky to have you."

"Let me know if you need anything. Anything at all."

The parade of kindness was overwhelming in its sincerity. By the time they made it outside into the bright sunshine, Ellie was crying again—happy tears this time, the kind that came from being accepted instead of judged.

Mabel was last in line, as she always seemed to be. She pulled Ellie into a hug that smelled like peppermint and hairspray and something floral that might have been lilac water—the same scent that clung to all of Ruth's things.

"Proud of you, baby girl," Mabel whispered fiercely into her ear. "Your grandmother would be so proud. You came back. You let people love you. That takes more courage than running ever did."

She pulled back, her eyes suspiciously bright behind her glasses. Then she turned to Caleb and poked him in the chest with one finger. "You take care of our girl, Sheriff. She's precious cargo."

"Yes, ma'am," Caleb said with appropriate seriousness.

"Both of them are precious cargo," Mabel added, her gaze

dropping pointedly to Ellie's belly. "That baby needs a good man in their life. Someone steady. Someone who shows up."

"Mabel—" Caleb's ears were turning red.

"I'm just saying what everyone's thinking." Mabel patted his cheek like he was still a teenager in her Sunday school class. "Now go on, get out of here before I start planning the baby shower. Though I am planning it, just so you know. June, you said? We'll do it in April. Give me your registry information when you have it."

Outside, the sun sparkled off fresh snow like crushed diamonds. Noah darted ahead to inspect icicles hanging from the church gutters, his sneakers blinking with every step. Caleb slowed their pace deliberately, giving Ellie time to catch her breath.

"You okay?" he asked for what had to be the twentieth time that morning.

She stopped walking completely, right there on the sidewalk in front of half the congregation filing out behind them. She looked up at him—at his concerned gray eyes and the worry line between his brows and the mouth that had kissed her so carefully last night.

"I'm terrified," she admitted honestly. "But I'm here. And I'm not running. And for the first time in months, I actually believe this might work. That maybe I can do this—have this baby, build a life, let people in. That maybe broken isn't the same as unfixable."

His smile was slow and warm, transforming his whole face. "Good. Because Noah's already planning your spot at the Christmas Eve dinner table, and Tripod staged a protest this morning when I suggested you might leave eventually. He carried your slipper around for twenty minutes like it was a security blanket."

Ellie laughed, the sound bright and genuine in the cold air. "I'm being strong-armed by an eight-year-old and a three-legged dog."

"Effective team," Caleb said with appropriate gravity.

"They've broken tougher nuts than you."

They started walking again, catching up to Noah who was now engaged in a detailed explanation to Mrs. Patterson about why snow was actually tiny pieces of clouds that got too heavy and fell down, a theory he'd apparently developed independently of any actual meteorological knowledge.

Halfway home, Noah ran back and grabbed both their hands, swinging between them like a pendulum, his grip sticky from the candy cane Pastor Mike had given him.

"Best Sunday ever," he declared with the certainty of someone whose Sundays usually involved sitting still for an hour and trying not to fidget.

Ellie looked at Caleb over Noah's head. He met her eyes, something fierce and tender blazing there that made her breath catch.

"Yeah," Caleb said quietly, his voice rough with emotion he wasn't trying to hide. "It really is."

And under the wide Colorado sky, with church bells still echoing behind them and a little boy's mittened hand in each of theirs, Ellie felt the last piece of her frozen heart crack wide open and start—finally, incredibly—to thaw.

The fear was still there. The uncertainty about Mark, about the future, about whether she deserved this kind of happiness. But it was smaller now, manageable, no longer the only thing she could feel.

Because beside it, growing stronger every day, was something else.

Hope. Real, fragile, terrifying hope that maybe—just maybe—she'd finally found where she belonged. Not despite being broken, but because broken was exactly what this place understood. This town. This man. This makeshift family that had claimed her before she'd even realized she was being claimed.

They turned onto Sparrow Lane, and the Victorian at the end of the street looked less sad now, less like a monument to loss and more like a project waiting to be tackled. Behind them, the town spread out like a postcard—white churches and red barns and smoke curling from chimneys into blue sky.

And as they climbed the steps to Caleb's porch—her porch now, at least for a while—she made herself a promise. She wouldn't run anymore.

Whatever came next—whether it was Mark making trouble, or legal battles, or the terrifying reality of becoming a mother—she would face it here. With Caleb beside her and Noah's boundless faith and this town's fierce, complicated love.

She was done running. It was time to stand and fight for the life she wanted. And maybe, if she was very brave and very lucky, she'd win.

Chapter 11

Monday brought chaos wrapped in tinsel and the distinct smell of livestock.

Ellie woke to the sound of Noah yelling "Daaaad! The donkey escaped again!" and the unmistakable clatter of hooves on hardwood floors echoing through the house like percussion in a very strange symphony.

She bolted upright, heart racing, her sleep-fogged brain taking several seconds to process the information. Donkey. Inside. How was there a donkey inside?

Then she remembered: live nativity rehearsal day. The church had borrowed a donkey named Kevin—current frontrunner in the name-the-nativity-animal contest—and two sheep who answered only to threats and bribes. They were supposed to arrive at the church at noon. It was barely eight in the morning.

By the time she threw on clothes and made it downstairs, Caleb was wrestling a small gray donkey toward the back door while Noah attempted to bribe it with Lucky Charms straight from the box. Tripod barked encouragement from the safety of the kitchen table, where he'd apparently taken refuge from the chaos.

"Morning," Caleb grunted, red-faced and breathing hard, his hair sticking up at odd angles. "Kevin decided the manger scene needed more authenticity. Or he's staging a coup. Hard to tell which."

Ellie pressed a hand to her mouth to keep from laughing, but it burst out anyway. "Do I want to know how he got inside?"

"Noah left the gate open when he went to check on Tripod. Kevin made executive decisions about his living arrangements." Caleb gave one more heave, and the donkey planted all four feet like they'd been nailed to the floor, staring at Caleb with ancient, judgmental eyes that suggested he found the sheriff's efforts both amusing and beneath his dignity.

The donkey swiveled his large head to look directly at Ellie, ears swiveling forward with interest.

She stepped forward slowly, hands extended in what she hoped was a non-threatening gesture. "Hey, Kevin. Want to be famous? Because you're about to star in the biggest production Estrella Ridge has seen in years."

Kevin considered this with the gravity of someone weighing career options. Then, to everyone's surprise, he took two steps toward Ellie and lowered his head, allowing her to scratch behind his ears.

Within thirty seconds he was following her like a large, opinionated dog, his hooves clicking on the hardwood as she led him toward the back door.

Caleb stared, his chest still heaving from exertion. "You're a donkey whisperer."

"Years of dealing with corporate clients," Ellie said solemnly, guiding Kevin out into the snow-covered backyard where a temporary pen had been set up. "Same skill set—stubborn, opinionated, secretly just want someone to listen to them."

They spent the next hour herding Kevin and the two sheep —Mabel had named them Mary and Joseph, which Pastor Mike said was "theologically confusing but we're going with it"—into the trailer Pastor Mike had parked in the driveway. The sheep were easier than expected, motivated primarily by the bucket of grain Noah carried like a Pied Piper of livestock.

Kevin required more negotiation. He would take three steps forward, then stop to stare at something only he could see. An interesting patch of snow. A bird in a distant tree. The existential question of whether he actually wanted to be in a nativity scene or if he'd rather stay here where the food was good and the small human gave him Lucky Charms.

Noah narrated the entire process like a nature documentary. "Here we see the majestic donkey in his natural habitat— Daddy's backyard—contemplating his career choices. Will he accept the role of a lifetime? Or will he choose freedom and breakfast cereal? The tension is palpable."

"Where did you learn the word 'palpable'?" Caleb asked, sounding both proud and exhausted.

"Mrs. Patterson's vocabulary calendar. Last week's word. I've been waiting to use it."

By the time the trailer finally pulled away with all three animals secured inside—Kevin staring out the back with a expression that suggested he was reconsidering his life choices—Ellie's coat was covered in donkey hair and hay, and she was laughing so hard her ribs hurt.

Caleb leaned against the porch rail, arms crossed, watching her with an expression she couldn't quite name. Something warm and wondering and slightly awed.

"What?" she asked, brushing straw off her sleeves.

"Nothing." He pushed off the rail and moved closer. "Just realizing you fit here better than you probably realize. Like you never left."

Her breath caught in her throat at the intensity in his voice.

He stepped closer still, voice dropping low so Noah—busy saying goodbye to Kevin through the trailer slats—wouldn't hear. "I talked to Pastor Mike after church yesterday. About the spare room. About you staying longer. He offered the parsonage if you want more space. Said the church would cover the costs until you're on your feet. But—"

"I like your spare room," she interrupted quickly. Too quickly. Her heart was hammering against her ribs.

His slow smile could have powered the entire town square. "Good. Because Noah's already moved your stuff into the bigger closet. And organized your toiletries by height in the bathroom. Kid works fast when he's motivated."

"He what?" Ellie's laugh was shaky with emotions she wasn't ready to name.

"I told him it was presumptuous. He said that's a big word that means 'I'm right and you know it.' Then he gave me a very detailed presentation about why you should stay forever, complete with charts he made on graph paper."

"Charts?"

"Bar graphs comparing your pancake-making skills to mine. Pie charts showing how much happier Tripod is since you arrived. A timeline of significant events, with your car accident marked as 'The Best Bad Thing That Ever Happened.' He's very thorough."

Ellie felt tears prick her eyes, the good kind that came from being wanted so completely it hurt. "That's—he's—"

"He's falling in love with you," Caleb said quietly. "We both are. Different kinds of love, obviously. His is the 'I want a mom and you're exactly what I didn't know I was praying for' kind. Mine is—" He stopped, ran a hand through his hair. "Mine is complicated. But it's real. And it's not going away just because it's inconvenient or scary or way too fast."

Before she could respond, the front door of the house next door banged open. Mabel appeared in a red sweater covered in appliqué bells that actually jingled when she moved.

"Caleb Brennan, is that animal hair all over your yard?" Her voice carried clear to the next county. "Lord have mercy, you're going to give the HOA a collective heart attack. Not that we have an HOA, but if we did, they'd be clutching their pearls."

"It's clean, Mabel," Caleb called back with admirable patience.

"And Ellie, honey!" Mabel's focus shifted with laser precision. "Emergency committee meeting at two. We need to finalize the festival schedule and someone—I'm not naming names but it rhymes with Barol Bean—tried to add a bake-off component and we need a tiebreaker vote."

Ellie wanted to say she had plans, that she needed rest, that she couldn't possibly handle another committee meeting. But the words died before they could form.

"I'll be there," she heard herself say.

Mabel beamed like she'd personally invented Christmas. "Excellent! And bring that handsome sheriff if he's free. We need someone to mediate if the bake-off discussion gets heated.

Last year Carol Jean threw a fruitcake at someone and it went through a window."

"It did not go through the window," Carol Jean's voice drifted from somewhere inside Mabel's house. "It *cracked* the window. There's a difference!"

"My point exactly!" Mabel called back, then winked at Ellie and Caleb. "Two o'clock. Don't be late. And Noah, baby, bring that dog inside before he freezes his remaining legs off!"

The door shut with a cheerful slam that somehow sounded triumphant.

Ellie turned back to Caleb, who was shaking his head with the resignation of someone who'd long ago accepted that Mabel would always win these battles.

"Does she ever take a day off?" Ellie asked.

"Christmas Day. And even then I'm not entirely sure. I think she just operates at a lower volume." He glanced at his watch. "I've got to head into the office for a few hours. Budget meeting with the county commissioners—exactly as exciting as it sounds. You okay here with Noah? He's off school now till after New Year's."

"We'll survive. Maybe work on his charts. Add some color coding."

"Don't encourage him. He already asked if he could present them at the festival committee meeting."

"That would be amazing."

"You're as bad as he is," Caleb accused, but he was smiling.

He leaned in, clearly intending to kiss her cheek—a casual goodbye, the kind of thing that would be appropriate in front of Noah. But she turned her head at the last second, and his lips caught the corner of her mouth instead.

They both froze.

Then Caleb cupped her face with one hand and kissed her properly—soft and sweet and achingly tender, the kind of kiss that promised more without demanding it. When he pulled back, his eyes were dark and intense.

"Tonight," he said, his voice rough. "After Noah goes to bed.

We talk. Really talk. About all of this. About what we're doing and where it's going and how fast is too fast."

She nodded, not trusting her voice.

He kissed her forehead once more, then headed for his truck, stopping to ruffle Noah's hair on the way. The truck pulled out of the driveway, and Ellie stood there on the porch, one hand pressed to her lips where she could still feel the warmth of him.

Noah appeared at her elbow, grinning up at her with gap-toothed knowing. "He kissed you."

"He did."

"On the lips."

"Sort of."

"Are you gonna marry him?"

Ellie choked on air. "Noah—"

"Because if you are, I have opinions about the wedding. Mrs. Mabel says for whoever Dad marries that I can be the ring bearer, but I think Tripod should do it. He's got three legs but he's very reliable. Plus he looks good in bow ties."

"Has Tripod worn bow ties before?"

"No, but I googled it and dogs can definitely pull it off. There are pictures."

Ellie laughed until tears streamed down her face, and Noah looked enormously pleased with himself.

Inside, the house felt different now—warmer, fuller, more like a home than a temporary refuge. Noah showed her his charts with pride, and they were indeed color-coded and surprisingly comprehensive for an eight-year-old's work.

"See, this graph shows how many times per day you smile now versus when you first got here," he explained, pointing to bars that climbed dramatically. "Day one you smiled maybe three times. Yesterday you smiled forty-seven times. I counted."

"You counted my smiles?"

"I'm a very attentive observer. It's a gift."

"That's a big word."

"Dad said that. He said it was good for a cop in the making."

They spent the morning making Christmas cookies—or

rather, Noah made cookies while Ellie provided moral support and watched as he ate approximately one-third of the dough. The kitchen became a disaster zone of flour and sprinkles and good intentions.

By late morning, Noah was dispatched next door to Mrs. Mabel's under the pretense of "helping" decorate cookies there too—a mission he accepted enthusiastically once he learned it involved icing, Christmas music, and the very real possibility of praise from an audience.

At two o'clock sharp, Ellie arrived at the courthouse meeting room to find the festival committee already in heated debate. Carol Jean and another woman whose name Ellie hadn't caught were arguing about whether gingerbread houses should be judged on taste or structural integrity.

"It's a bake-off, not an engineering competition!" Carol Jean insisted.

"But presentation matters! Would you rather eat an ugly cake or a pretty one?"

"I'd rather eat a delicious cake, regardless of its aesthetic appeal!"

Mabel banged her candy cane gavel—yes, she had an actual gavel shaped like a candy cane—on the table. "Order! Ellie's here. She'll decide."

All eyes turned to Ellie expectantly.

She looked at the two women, at their passionate faces, at the other committee members trying hard not to laugh. Then she channeled every corporate meeting she'd ever mediated.

"Both," she said firmly. "Two categories. Best taste, best presentation. Two separate prizes. We double the winners and everyone goes home happy."

The room went silent.

Then Mabel started clapping, and everyone joined in.

"This is why we needed professional marketing expertise," Mabel declared. "Meeting adjourned. Ellie, stay after. We need to discuss your role in the live nativity."

Two hours later, Ellie had been assigned to:

- Narrate the live nativity (because apparently her "city voice carries well")
- Judge the gingerbread competition (both categories)
- Organize the children's choir performance
- And somehow wrangle Kevin the donkey into behaving during the actual Christmas Eve performance

She stumbled out of the meeting room feeling like she'd been conscripted into something much larger than a small-town Christmas festival. But she was also smiling. Because for the first time in years—maybe ever—she felt needed. Not for what she could provide financially or professionally. But for who she was. For her skills and her presence and the simple fact that she'd shown up.

That evening, after Noah had been tucked in with the reindeer book and three different promises that yes, Ellie would still be there in the morning, she and Caleb sat on the couch in front of the fire.

He'd changed into sweatpants and that ancient Army t-shirt again. She wore yoga pants and one of his hoodies that she'd borrowed and had no intention of returning. The sleeves hung past her hands and it smelled like him—pine and coffee and something indefinably safe.

"So," he said, turning to face her, one arm stretched across the back of the couch. "We should probably talk about what's happening here."

"Probably," she agreed, her heart starting to race.

"I meant what I said this morning," he said quietly. "About falling in love with you—about realizing it never really stopped." His voice was steady, sure. "I know the timing is a mess. I know you're carrying more than anyone should have to. But I'm done pretending this is something smaller than it is."

Ellie swallowed hard. "I'm falling too. Deeper. Which terrifies me. Because the last time I fell, I fell for someone who hurt me. Someone who made me question my own judgment, my own worth. And I don't—I can't—"

"I'm not him," Caleb said quietly. "I will never be him. I will never raise my hand to you. Never make you feel small. Never make you choose between me and anything else you love."

"I know that. Logically I know that. But there's this part of me that's just... waiting for the other shoe to drop. Waiting for you to realize I'm too much work. Too much baggage. Too complicated."

He reached for her hand, threading their fingers together. "Ellie, I'm a widower with a son who prays for robot legs and thinks donkeys make good house pets. I work long hours in a job that's sometimes dangerous. I have bad days when I miss Sarah so much I can barely function. I have a mother-in-law who calls every Sunday to check on Noah and sometimes cries on the phone. I am the definition of complicated."

"That's different—"

"It's not. We're both carrying weight. We're both scared. But here's what I know—we can carry it together better than we can carry it alone. And I'd rather risk getting hurt again than miss the chance at this. At you. At us."

Ellie felt tears sliding down her cheeks. "What if Mark causes trouble? What if he shows up and makes a scene? What if he tries to use the baby as leverage somehow, even though he doesn't want—"

"Then we handle it. Together. You're not alone in this anymore, Ellie. Whatever he throws at you, he's throwing at both of us now. And I'm pretty good at handling trouble."

She laughed wetly. "You're the sheriff. You're supposed to say that."

"I'm saying it as a man who loves you. Who wants to protect you and your baby. Who wants to be there for all of it—the good parts and the hard parts and everything in between."

He pulled her closer, and she went willingly, tucking herself against his side. His arm came around her shoulders, holding her secure.

"I'm scared," she whispered against his chest.

"Me too," he admitted. "But I'm more scared of not trying."

They sat like that for a long time, the fire crackling, the Christmas tree lights blinking their steady pattern. Outside, snow began to fall again, soft and quiet.

"Okay," Ellie said finally. "Okay. Let's try. Let's see where this goes. But slowly—"

"We're way past slowly," Caleb interrupted with a huff of laughter. "You're living in my house, mothering my son, and I've kissed you approximately eight times in three days. Slowly left the building sometime Friday night."

"Fine. Let's try honestly then. No pretending things are fine when they're not. No hiding when things get hard."

"Deal." He kissed the top of her head. "For the record? This —you here, us talking, Noah sleeping upstairs happy for the first time in months—this is the best thing to happen to me since Sarah died. And I'm not letting fear take it away."

Ellie tilted her face up to look at him, at the firelight dancing across his features, at the absolute certainty in his eyes.

Then she kissed him, deep and sure and full of promise.

When they broke apart, both breathing hard, she whispered, "I love you too. Just so you know. It's terrifying and probably insane and way too fast, but it's true."

His answering smile was incandescent. "Best Christmas present ever."

"It's not even Christmas yet."

"Early present, then. I'll take it."

"I left because I thought wanting more meant going farther," Ellie said quietly. "I thought this town was too small for me, that staying would mean shrinking. But the world didn't get bigger when I left—it just got louder. And emptier."

She met his eyes. "I'm not afraid of staying anymore. I'm afraid of running again and calling it courage."

They stayed up late talking—about everything and nothing, about hopes and fears and what came next. About the baby and Noah and how they'd navigate the complicated reality of blending lives that had been separate for so long.

And when Ellie finally climbed the stairs to her room—to the guest room that felt less like a guest room every day—she felt lighter than she had in months.

Scared, yes. Uncertain about the future, absolutely. But no longer alone. And that made all the difference.

Chapter 12

Tuesday dawned gray and heavy, the kind of sky that promised more snow and fewer answers.

Ellie woke to an empty house. A note on the coffeemaker—Caleb's handwriting, bold and slanted—read: *Took Noah to his friend's, then court in Durango. Back by lunch. Don't let Tripod eat the Christmas tree. He's been eyeing the lower branches. Love, C*

The "Love, C" was written firmly this time, no scratching out, no second-guessing. Just confident declaration.

She stood there holding the note for a long time, her thumb rubbing over the word "love" until the ink started to smudge. The house felt wrong in its quietness after days of constant noise and laughter. Too still. Too silent. The kind of silence that let unwanted thoughts creep in.

She showered, dressed in her most comfortable clothes—leggings and an oversized sweater that was definitely Caleb's but he hadn't asked for back. Her phone sat on the bathroom counter, screen dark and innocent.

Three days since Mark's last call. Three days of radio silence that felt more ominous than reassuring.

Men like Mark didn't give up. They regrouped. Strategized. Came back harder.

She picked up the phone with reluctant fingers and checked her email, something she'd been avoiding since Friday. Her inbox was a disaster—127 unread messages, most of them junk. But three stood out, all from the same sender.

Mark's lawyer.

Her stomach dropped like an elevator with cut cables.

She opened the first one, dated Saturday:

Ms. Freeman, This is the third attempt to reach you regarding the property settlement. Mr. Freeman needs a response to his latest offer by December 20th or we will be forced to proceed with litigation. Please confirm receipt of this email and your intentions moving forward.

The second, Sunday:

Ms. Freeman, Your continued silence is concerning. Mr. Freeman is prepared to be reasonable, but that window is closing. The longer you delay, the more expensive this becomes for everyone involved. Please respond immediately.

The third, yesterday:

Ms. Freeman, Since you are not responding to emails or phone calls, we will be serving papers at your last known address in Las Vegas. If you have relocated, please provide updated contact information immediately to avoid complications.

Ellie's hands shook as she set the phone down. Papers. They were serving papers. Which meant Mark knew—or would soon know—that she wasn't at the Las Vegas house anymore. Would know she'd left the state. And once he knew that, he'd want to know where.

How long before he tracked her here? How long before he showed up in Estrella Ridge, making threats, causing scenes, destroying this fragile peace she'd found?

She pressed both hands to her face, trying to breathe through the rising panic.

Call your lawyer, she told herself. *That's what you pay her for. Call Rebecca.*

But it was barely eight in the morning. Rebecca wouldn't be in her office yet.

Ellie forced herself to make coffee, to eat a piece of toast she didn't want, to go through the motions of a normal morning. Tripod watched her from his spot by the fireplace, his head tilted like he knew something was wrong.

At 8:30, her phone rang. Rebecca's number.

"I was just about to call you," Ellie answered, her voice shakier than she wanted.

"Good, because we need to talk." Rebecca's voice was brisk, professional, the tone she used when things were serious. "Mark's lawyer filed a motion yesterday. They're claiming you've violated the terms of the temporary separation agreement by relocating without notification. It's bull—the agreement says you can live wherever you want as long as you maintain contact, which you have. But they're using it as leverage to push for a faster settlement."

"What does that mean?"

"It means they want to scare you into accepting their offer. The house for him, he pays you out for your equity but at a reduced rate because you 'abandoned' the property. They're also trying to argue that your relocation proves you're unstable, which could impact—"

"The baby," Ellie finished, her voice hollow. "He said he didn't want anything to do with the baby."

"He doesn't. But his lawyer is smart enough to know that the threat of a custody fight will make you more compliant. They don't actually want custody—they want you scared enough to take a bad deal."

Ellie sank into a kitchen chair, her legs suddenly unreliable. "What do I do?"

"First, don't panic. This is standard aggressive litigation tactics. Second, I need your current address so I can update our records and notify opposing counsel that you're in compliance with all requirements. Third, we need to respond to their motion by Friday. I'll handle the legal arguments, but I need you to document everything—where you're staying, why you left Nevada, anything that shows you're being responsible and stable."

"I'm staying with—" Ellie stopped, unsure how to explain. "I'm staying with a friend. The local sheriff. In Estrella Ridge, Colorado."

There was a pause on the line. "The sheriff?"

"It's not—we're not—" Except they were. "It's complicated."

"Complicated how?" Rebecca's voice had shifted into protective mode. "Ellie, if you're in a new relationship, we need to be very careful about how we present that. Mark's lawyer will use it to paint you as unstable, as jumping from one man to another—"

"Caleb is nothing like Mark," Ellie said fiercely. "He's kind and stable and he's been nothing but supportive. He has a son. He's a widower. He's a sheriff, for God's sake. He's the definition of responsible."

"I believe you. But that's not how opposing counsel will spin it." Rebecca sighed. "Okay, here's what we do. You're staying with family friends while dealing with a family property issue—your grandmother's estate. That's true, right? You inherited property there?"

"Yes. Grandma Ruth's house."

"Perfect. You're handling estate matters while the Las Vegas property settlement is pending. You're in temporary housing with long-time family friends while your grandmother's house undergoes necessary repairs. You're establishing prenatal care locally. You're doing everything a responsible parent-to-be should do. The fact that you're romantically involved with your host is nobody's business unless it becomes relevant to custody, which it won't because Mark doesn't want custody."

Ellie felt some of the panic recede. This was why she paid Rebecca's astronomical hourly rate—the woman could find solid ground in quicksand.

"I need you to email me the details," Rebecca continued. "Current address, contact information for your host—Sheriff, what's his name?"

"Caleb Brennan. Sheriff of Estrella Ridge."

"Good. Having a law enforcement officer vouch for your stability is actually helpful. I also need the name of your new OB, proof that you've established care. Have you seen a doctor there yet?"

"No, I have… had… an appointment scheduled in Las Vegas for next week—"

"Cancel it. Establish local care immediately. Today if possible. I need documentation that you're being proactive about prenatal care. Find a doctor, get an appointment, get it in writing."

"Okay." Ellie was writing notes on the back of an envelope.

"What about Mark? Can he come here? Is there anything stopping him?"

"The restraining order is still in effect, so technically he can't contact you directly. But he can be in the same town—the order is about contact, not proximity. If he shows up, don't engage. Call the local police immediately. Have them document everything. And Ellie?" Rebecca's voice softened slightly. "You're doing the right thing. You got yourself safe, you're building a support system. Don't let his lawyer make you doubt that."

After they hung up, Ellie sat at the kitchen table staring at her notes. The list of things to do felt overwhelming:

- Email Rebecca with current details
- Find a local OB, make an appointment
- Document everything about her living situation
- Prepare for the possibility that Mark might show up
- Try not to have a complete breakdown

She was on task three when the front door opened. Caleb's voice called out, "Ellie? You here?"

She checked the clock—only ten-thirty. He wasn't supposed to be back until lunch.

He appeared in the kitchen doorway still in his uniform, snowflakes melting on his shoulders. One look at her face and his expression shifted from casual to concerned in half a second.

"What happened?"

"Mark's lawyer filed a motion. They're trying to say I violated the separation agreement by leaving Las Vegas. My lawyer says it's leverage, that they're trying to scare me into a bad settlement, but—" Her voice cracked. "They're threatening a custody fight. Even though Mark doesn't want the baby. They're just using it to —"

Caleb was across the kitchen in three strides, pulling her out of the chair and into his arms. She pressed her face against his chest, trying not to fall apart completely.

"Okay," he said, his voice calm and steady even though she could feel his heart racing. "Okay. Tell me what your lawyer said. All of it."

She did, in halting sentences, while he held her and listened without interrupting. When she finished, he was quiet for a moment, thinking.

"Your lawyer's right," he said finally. "This is intimidation tactics. But we can handle it. First, Doc Martinez—she's the OB I mentioned. I called her on the way home, told her we had a situation. She can see you this afternoon at two if you can make it."

"You called her?"

"Court ended early, and I had a feeling—" He pulled back to look at her. "I had a feeling something was going on. You were too quiet this morning. So I called in a favor."

Ellie felt tears sting her eyes. "Thank you."

"Second, you need to document your living situation. I'll write a statement as a law enforcement officer about your presence here, your stability, your engagement with the community. Pastor Mike will do the same. So will Mabel—woman's a menace, but she's respected. Between the three of us, we can establish that you're not hiding or running. You're building a life."

"Rebecca said the same thing."

"Your lawyer sounds smart. Listen to her." He cupped her face in both hands, his thumbs brushing away tears. "And Ellie? If Mark shows up here, he's dealing with me. Not just as your—" he hesitated over the word, then committed "—your boyfriend. But as sheriff. He comes anywhere near you, makes any threats, causes any trouble, he's going to learn very quickly that this isn't Las Vegas."

"I don't want you to get in trouble because of me—"

"I won't. Everything I do will be by the book. But the book gives me a lot of options when someone violates a restraining order in my jurisdiction." His voice was hard, flat, the sheriff voice she'd heard him use on the phone with county officials. "He wants to play games? He can play them with me."

She kissed him then, hard and desperate, pouring all her fear and gratitude into it. He kissed her back just as fiercely, one hand sliding into her hair, the other splayed wide on her lower back.

When they broke apart, both breathing hard, he rested his forehead against hers.

"We're going to get through this," he said firmly. "All of it. The lawyers, the settlement, the custody threats. We're going to document everything, follow every rule, and show that you're doing exactly what a good parent does—protecting your child and building a stable life."

"What if it's not enough?"

"Then we fight harder. But Ellie—" he waited until she looked at him "—you're not alone in this. Whatever he throws at us, we face it together. He doesn't get to scare you into giving up on this life. On us. Not without going through me first."

She nodded, not trusting her voice.

"Now," he said, shifting back to practical matters, "let's get you some lunch. Then we'll go see Doc Martinez. After that, we'll sit down and write out everything your lawyer needs. One step at a time. We've got this."

They made sandwiches together, the domestic routine soothing in its normalcy. Caleb told her about court—a custody hearing for a different family, messy and sad but resolved peacefully in the end. She told him about Noah's charts and the committee meeting chaos.

At two o'clock, they walked three blocks to Doc Martinez's office, a converted Victorian house painted cheerful yellow. The waiting room smelled like lavender and old magazines. Carol Jean was behind the reception desk—apparently she worked here part-time between her flower shop duties.

"Ellie Freeman!" She came around the desk to hug her. "Doc's excited to meet you. She delivered Caleb, you know. And Sarah. And Noah. Woman's delivered half the town at this point."

Doc Martinez herself was sixty, Hispanic, with salt-and-pepper hair in a long braid and the kind of capable hands that made you trust her immediately. Her office was covered in baby photos—decades of them, a wall of proof that she was good at her job.

"So," she said after the initial examination was done, "you're fourteen weeks, baby looks perfect, heartbeat's strong at 162. Everything measures right where it should. You're doing great, mama."

"Really?" Ellie's voice was small.

"Really. I know you're dealing with a lot of stress—Caleb gave me the basics. But your body is doing what it needs to do. Baby's protected. You just need to protect yourself too. Eat well, rest when you can, and lean on your support system." She glanced meaningfully at Caleb, who was sitting in the chair next to the examination table, holding Ellie's hand. "Which it looks like you're doing."

She printed out ultrasound photos—grainy black and white images that showed a tiny profile, a perfect curve of spine, hands near face. "Baby's measuring right on track. Due date looks like June 18th, give or take. Here's your next appointment—two weeks from today. And here—" she handed over a thick folder "—is all the documentation your lawyer will need. Established prenatal care, healthy pregnancy, stable living situation. You're doing everything right, Ellie."

Walking out of the office with Caleb, ultrasound photos clutched in her hand, Ellie felt something shift inside her. Not all the fear disappearing—that would take time. But underneath it, something stronger was taking root.

Determination.

Mark could threaten all he wanted. His lawyer could file motions and make demands. But she wasn't the same scared woman who'd left Nevada three months ago.

She had a plan. She had support. She had people who loved her and were willing to fight for her.

And she had proof, right here in her hands, that she was building the life her baby deserved.

When they got back to the house, Noah was already home from his friend's—Mabel had picked him up, apparently, and fed him cookies and gossip in equal measure.

"Ellie!" He launched himself at her. "Mrs. Mabel says you went to the baby doctor! Can I see pictures? Does the baby look like a baby yet or is it still just like a blob? Jake Hensley says babies look like aliens at first but I think that's probably not true because God wouldn't make alien babies, right?"

She showed him the ultrasound photos, and his eyes went wide with wonder.

"That's a real baby," he breathed. "Like, a real actual person."

"It is."

"Does it have a name yet?"

"Not yet. Won't know if it's a boy or a girl for a few more weeks."

"Can I help pick the name? I have ideas. Good ones. Like if it's a boy, Thunder. Or if it's a girl, Rainbow. Or for either, we could name it Taco. Everybody loves Tacos."

Caleb covered his face with both hands. "Ellie is not naming the baby Taco."

"Why not? It's a great name!"

"It's a food."

"So is Olive. And Ginger. And Sage. Mrs. Patterson told me those are all names."

"I'll... take it under advisement," Ellie said, trying not to laugh.

That night, after Noah was asleep and the house was quiet, Ellie sat at the kitchen table with her laptop while Caleb wrote his statement for her lawyer. She organized documents, drafted emails, built the paper trail that would prove she was stable, responsible, and doing everything right.

And when exhaustion finally overtook her and she closed the laptop, Caleb pulled her into his arms on the couch.

"You did good today," he murmured into her hair. "I'm proud of you."

"I haven't done anything yet. Just paperwork."

"You didn't run. You didn't hide. You faced it head-on. That's huge."

She tilted her face up to look at him. "I couldn't have done it without you."

"You could have. But I'm glad you didn't have to."

They stayed like that, wrapped around each other, while the fire burned low and the Christmas tree lights blinked their steady pattern.

Tomorrow would bring more challenges. More emails from lawyers, more preparations, more waiting for the other shoe to drop. But tonight, she was safe. She was loved. She was exactly where she needed to be. And that was enough. For now, it was more than enough. It was everything.

Chapter 13

Wednesday morning arrived with fresh snow and a sense of impending doom that Ellie couldn't quite shake.

She'd slept fitfully, dreams full of courtrooms and Mark's cold smile and endless hallways where she ran but never got anywhere. When she finally gave up on sleep at six-thirty, she found Caleb already in the kitchen, dressed in his uniform, nursing coffee that was probably his second or third cup judging by the shadows under his eyes.

"Couldn't sleep either?" she asked, padding into the kitchen in bare feet and his borrowed sweatshirt.

"Noah had a nightmare around three. Took a while to get him settled." He poured her a cup of coffee, added the right amount of sugar without asking. "He's worried about you. Kids pick up on more than we think they do."

Guilt twisted in her stomach. "I'm sorry. I didn't mean to—"

"Hey." He set down his mug and pulled her into a hug. "Don't. You're dealing with a genuine threat. You're allowed to be stressed. And Noah's tough. He just wanted reassurance that you weren't leaving."

"What did you tell him?"

"The truth. That you're staying. That we're all in this together. That sometimes grown-ups have to deal with hard things, but that doesn't mean the family falls apart." He pressed a kiss to the top of her head. "He asked if the baby's daddy was coming to take you away. I told him no. That you're safe here, and we're going to make sure it stays that way."

Ellie's eyes burned with tears she was getting tired of crying. "You're too good at this. At all of it."

"Years of practice with a kid who asks hard questions." He pulled back to look at her. "Listen, I have to go in early today. Meeting with the county prosecutor about a case. But I'll have my phone on me all day. Anything happens, anything at all, you call. Don't hesitate."

"I will."

"And Mabel's expecting you at the church at ten for nativity rehearsal. Apparently Kevin has been practicing his entrance and needs your 'calming influence.'" His mouth quirked. "Her words, not mine."

"A donkey needs my calming influence. This is my life now."

"Could be worse. Could be two donkeys."

After Caleb left for work and Noah for school—Mabel picking him up again with promises of hot chocolate and "educational Christmas activities" that probably involved excessive amounts of glitter—Ellie stood in the quiet house trying to decide what to do with herself.

Her phone buzzed. A text from Rebecca:

Got your documentation. Perfect. Filing our response today. Also—heads up. Mark's lawyer called this morning. He wants to settle. Meeting tomorrow in Las Vegas if you can make it. I think we rattled him with the sheriff's statement.

Ellie's heart kicked into overdrive. Tomorrow. Las Vegas. Facing Mark across a conference table.

She typed back: *Can it be a video call? I don't want to go back to Nevada. Not yet.*

Rebecca's response was immediate: *I'll push for it. Stand by.*

Ellie set down her phone and pressed both hands to her belly, feeling the slight swell that was becoming more pronounced every day. "What do you think, little one? Can we do this?"

The baby gave a tiny flutter, like a butterfly testing its wings.

"I'll take that as a yes."

At ten o'clock she arrived at the church to find absolute chaos. Kevin the donkey had apparently decided that the stable set wasn't architecturally sound and had kicked over two hay bales and a cardboard manger. The sheep—Mary and Joseph, because Mabel's theological confusion continued unchecked— had eaten through their restraints and were currently investigating the church kitchen with intense interest.

Pastor Mike stood in the middle of the sanctuary looking like a man questioning all his life choices.

"Ellie! Thank God." He grabbed her arm like a drowning man grabbing a life preserver. "Kevin refuses to stand where he's supposed to stand. Mary—the sheep, not the virgin—has eaten three hymnals. And Joseph—again, the sheep—has apparently fallen in love with Carol Jean's coat and won't let go of it."

"Where's the nativity coordinator?"

"You're looking at him. Mabel was supposed to help but she got called away for an emergency at the senior center. Something about a gingerbread house collapsing and structural recriminations."

Ellie bit back a laugh. "Okay. Let me see what I can do."

It took two hours, three buckets of grain, and more patience than she knew she possessed, but eventually Kevin was standing in approximately the right spot, the sheep were secured with reinforced leads, and Pastor Mike looked slightly less like he was planning to fake his own death and move to Tahiti.

"You're a miracle worker," he said with genuine awe. "How did you get Kevin to cooperate?"

"I promised him first pick of the Christmas Eve cookies. And I may have sung to him."

"You sang to a donkey."

"'O Holy Night.' He seemed to like it. Either that or he was judging my pitch, hard to tell with donkeys."

Pastor Mike laughed so hard he had to sit down in a pew. "Ruth would have loved this. She always said Christmas was supposed to be a little chaotic. That the original nativity probably involved stubborn donkeys and inconvenient sheep and Mary absolutely losing her mind at Joseph for booking the worst hotel in Bethlehem."

Ellie smiled despite her stress. "That sounds like Grandma Ruth."

"She talked about you, you know. After you left. Never stopped hoping you'd come home." His voice was gentle, careful. "She knew about Mark. About what he was like. She prayed for you every single day. Prayed you'd find your way back when you were ready."

Ellie's throat closed completely. "She never said anything. Never called, never—"

"She didn't want to push. Said you needed space to figure things out. But she never stopped loving you. Never stopped hoping." He paused, then added quietly, "She'd be so proud of you right now. Proud that you got yourself safe. Proud that you're building something good here."

Ellie had to excuse herself to the bathroom to cry, which was becoming an unfortunate habit.

When she emerged, red-eyed but composed, Pastor Mike pretended not to notice. "So, Christmas Eve. You'll be narrating the live nativity, which mostly means reading the Luke passage and trying not to laugh when Kevin inevitably does something ridiculous. Think you can handle it?"

"I narrated a product launch in front of three hundred people once. I can handle a donkey."

"That's the spirit."

Her phone buzzed as she was leaving the church. Rebecca.

Video call approved for tomorrow, 2pm. I'll send you the link. Be somewhere quiet with good internet. And Ellie—we're going to end this. Mark's lawyer knows they don't have a case. They're going to push for their best offer and we're going to push back until it's fair. You're going to walk away from this free.

Free. The word felt foreign, impossible.

But also—for the first time—real.

She was walking back to Caleb's house, lost in thought, when a car pulled up beside her. Not a local car—too sleek, too expensive. A black BMW with Nevada plates.

Her blood turned to ice.

The driver's window rolled down.

Mark.

He looked exactly the same—sharp suit, expensive watch, that smile that used to make her heart flutter and now made her stomach turn. His hair was perfectly styled, his cologne probably cost more than most people's monthly rent.

"Ellie." His voice was smooth, practiced. "We need to talk."

She stopped walking but didn't approach the car. Her hand was already fumbling for her phone in her pocket. "You're violating the restraining order."

"I'm not threatening you. I'm not even getting out of the car. I'm just talking." He spread his hands in a gesture of innocence that made her skin crawl. "Five minutes. That's all I'm asking."

"I have nothing to say to you. My lawyer will talk to your lawyer tomorrow."

"Come on, El. Don't be like this. We can work this out like adults without dragging it through mediation." His tone was reasonable, persuasive—the same tone he'd used to convince her that she was overreacting when she'd asked about the charges on their credit card from the hotel where his "conference" had been. "I'm willing to be generous. You keep the house, I'll buy you out at full market value. You drop the child support claim—since we both know I'm not interested in being a father—and we're done. Clean break."

"That's not what your lawyer offered."

His smile thinned. "My lawyer is a snake who bills by the hour. I'm trying to save us both money and time. Just sign the papers, Ellie. Move on with your life. Isn't that what you want?"

"What I want is for you to leave. Now."

"You're being unreasonable." His voice sharpened, the mask slipping slightly. "I'm trying to be nice here. Trying to give you what you want. But if you keep pushing—"

"If I keep pushing, what?" She was surprised by how steady her voice was, how calm she sounded when inside she was screaming. "You'll what, Mark? Threaten me? Sue for custody of a baby you don't even want? Show up at my grandmother's town and harass me?"

"I'm not harassing you. I'm trying to have a conversation."

"This conversation is over." She had her phone out now, was dialing with shaking fingers. "You need to leave. Right now."

"Ellie—"

"Leave. Or I'm calling the sheriff, and you can explain to him why you're violating a restraining order."

Something ugly flashed across his face. "The local sheriff? Really? That's who you're running to? Small-town cop who probably peaked in high school?"

He paused, head tilting slightly as something clicked into place. His mouth twisted. "Oh."

The word was soft. Dangerous.

"Your high school boyfriend," he said slowly, savoring it. "The one you never quite got over. Guess I should've known— girls like you always circle back to what made them feel special before they learned how to want more."

"Better than running from my own husband because I was afraid he'd put me through a wall."

The words were out before she could stop them, raw and honest and angrier than she'd let herself be in months.

Mark's face went dark. "I never—"

"You grabbed me hard enough to bruise. You pushed me into the kitchen counter. You punched a hole in the bedroom wall six inches from my head. You destroyed my phone when I tried to call my sister. Don't you dare tell me what you never did."

"You're exaggerating. You're making me sound like—"

"Like an abuser?" Her voice was shaking now, but not with fear. With rage. "If it walks like a duck, Mark."

A truck pulled up behind Mark's BMW—Caleb's sheriff's vehicle, lights flashing.

Mark's expression shifted instantly—the angry mask replaced by smooth charm. "Sheriff. Good timing. I was just leaving."

Caleb got out of his truck with deliberate slowness, one hand resting casually on his belt near his weapon. Not threatening, just present. His face was absolutely neutral, professionally blank.

"License and registration, please."

"I wasn't speeding—"

"You were stopped in a no-parking zone, harassing a resident who has a restraining order against you. License and registration. Now."

Mark's jaw clenched, but he produced the documents. Caleb

took his time examining them, running them through his system, making Mark wait.

Finally he handed them back. "Mr. Freeman. Here's what's going to happen. You're going to leave Estrella Ridge immediately. You're not going to contact Ms. Freeman directly. You're not going to drive past her residence. You're not going to show up at her place of work or anywhere else she might be. All contact goes through lawyers. Are we clear?"

"I have a right to be here. This is a public street."

"And I have a right to enforce the restraining order that says you maintain a distance of 500 feet from Ms. Freeman. Right now you're about fifty feet away. So unless you want me to arrest you for violation of a court order, I suggest you start your car and drive back to the airport."

"You can't—"

"I can. And I will." Caleb's voice was flat, utterly without emotion. "Test me. Please. I'd love the paperwork."

Mark looked at Ellie, something calculating in his eyes. "This isn't over. The settlement meeting is tomorrow. My lawyer expects you there."

"My lawyer will be there. Via video call. I'll be somewhere safe, far away from you."

He looked like he wanted to say more, but Caleb shifted slightly—nothing aggressive, just a subtle movement that said *I'm here and I'm not going anywhere.*

Mark started his car. "You're making a mistake, Ellie. You could have handled this reasonably."

Then he was gone, the BMW's engine purring as it disappeared down the street.

The second he was out of sight, Ellie's knees gave out. Caleb caught her before she hit the ground, pulling her against his chest.

"I've got you. You're okay. He's gone."

"How did you—how did you know—"

"Mabel called. Said she saw a car she didn't recognize pull up beside you. Small-town surveillance system at work." He was already pulling out his phone. "I'm calling this in. Documenting everything. Time, location, what he said. You did perfect, Ellie. Got him on record violating the restraining order."

"I should have—I shouldn't have engaged—"

"You stood your ground. You were strong. And you got him to incriminate himself. Your lawyer is going to have a field day with this."

She was shaking so hard she couldn't stand. He half-carried her to his truck, settled her in the passenger seat, cranked the heat.

"We're going to document everything you remember him saying, we're going to call your lawyer, and then we're going to lock the doors and not think about him until tomorrow."

"The settlement meeting—"

"Will happen over video call with your lawyer present and me sitting right beside you. He doesn't get anywhere near you again. I promise you that."

By the time they got back to the house, Ellie had stopped shaking but felt hollowed out, exhausted in a way that had nothing to do with physical tiredness.

Caleb called Rebecca while Ellie sat at the kitchen table, and she listened as he gave a professional, detailed account of everything that had happened. Time stamps, exact location, witness reports from Mabel and two other neighbors who'd seen the interaction.

When he hung up, he relayed the message. "Your lawyer says this is huge. Clear violation of the restraining order. She's filing an emergency motion to modify it to include the entire county. She's also pretty sure Mark's lawyer is going to be very motivated to settle quickly and quietly now, before this becomes a criminal matter."

"So tomorrow—"

"Tomorrow we end this. Once and for all." He crouched in front of her chair, taking both her hands. "You did so good today, Ellie. I know it doesn't feel like it. I know you're scared. But you faced him, you stood your ground, and you got proof of exactly what kind of man he is. That takes incredible courage."

"I just want it to be over. I want to stop being scared. Stop looking over my shoulder. Stop waiting for him to show up and ruin everything."

"After tomorrow, you won't have to. We're going to end this, get you free, and then you can focus on what matters—you, the baby, building the life you want... Us."

Ellie's breath caught. *Us.*

The word settled somewhere deep and unfamiliar—not frightening, exactly, but heavy with possibility. She didn't trust herself to answer right away, afraid anything she said might either break the moment or reveal how much she wanted to believe him.

That evening, after Noah was in bed and the house was quiet, Ellie sat on the couch wrapped in blankets while Caleb built up the fire. She felt fragile, like glass that had been cracked but not yet shattered.

"Talk to me," Caleb said, settling beside her. "What are you thinking?"

"That I let him control me for so long. Let him make me small. Let him convince me that I was the problem, that I was too sensitive, too dramatic, too needy. And today, facing him—" She swallowed hard. "It reminded me of who I was before him. Someone who didn't back down. Someone who fought for what mattered."

"You're still that person. You never stopped being her."

"I forgot for a while."

"Then remember now. Remember that you're strong enough to leave. Strong enough to protect your baby. Strong enough to build a new life in a place that's not always easy or convenient." He pulled her closer. "Remember that you're the woman who can calm stubborn donkeys and wrangle church ladies and stand up to the man who tried to break you. Remember that you're exactly as strong as you need to be."

She turned to look at him, at the firelight playing across his features, at the absolute certainty in his eyes.

"I love you," she said. "I know we've said it before, but I need you to know—I really love you. Not just because you saved me or protected me or gave me a place to stay. I love you because you see me. All of me. The broken parts and the scared parts and the parts that are still learning how to be strong again. And you love all of it."

His kiss was gentle, reverent, like she was something holy. "I love you too. Every stubborn, brave, beautiful part of you."

They stayed like that for a long time, wrapped around each other, the fire crackling and the Christmas tree lights blinking their steady pattern.

Tomorrow would bring the settlement meeting. Would bring the chance to finally close this chapter of her life.

But tonight, she was safe. She was loved. She was exactly where she needed to be.

And when Caleb carried her upstairs to bed—to his bed this time, not the guest room—and held her while she fell into exhausted sleep, she dreamed not of courtrooms and cold smiles.

She dreamed of summer days and baby laughter and a future that was finally, blessedly hers.

Free. The word settled over her like a benediction. Tomorrow she would fight for it. Tonight, she would rest in it. And either way, she was not alone. Not anymore.

Chapter 14

Thursday morning arrived with crystalline clarity—the sky so blue it hurt to look at, the sun reflecting off snow with blinding intensity.

Ellie woke in Caleb's bed, wrapped in his arms, the unfamiliar weight of him beside her both comforting and terrifying. They hadn't done anything beyond sleep, but the intimacy of sharing space, of his slow breathing in her ear, of waking to his hand splayed protectively over her belly—it felt more significant than anything physical could have been.

"You're thinking too loud," he mumbled against her hair, voice rough with sleep. "I can hear the gears turning from here."

"Sorry. Didn't mean to wake you."

"I was already awake. Just enjoying the view." He pressed a kiss to her shoulder. "How are you feeling? About today?"

"Terrified. Ready. Angry. Hopeful. All of it at once." She turned to face him, their noses almost touching on the shared pillow. "What if he doesn't agree to reasonable terms? What if this drags on for months?"

"Then it drags on, and we deal with it. But Ellie—after yesterday, after he violated the restraining order with witnesses and documentation—his lawyer knows they're in trouble. They're going to want this settled quietly before it becomes a criminal case that ends up in the papers." His thumb traced her cheekbone. "You hold all the cards now. You just have to be brave enough to play them."

Downstairs, they found Noah already awake, eating cereal at the kitchen table while watching videos on Caleb's tablet. He looked up when they entered, his expression too knowing for an eight-year-old.

"Did Ellie sleep in your room, Daddy?"

Caleb didn't even blink. "Yes. She had a hard day yesterday

and needed extra support. Sometimes adults need comfort too."

"Like when I have nightmares and you let me sleep in your bed?"

"Exactly like that."

Noah considered this, seemed satisfied with the logic. "Okay. Can we have pancakes? The regular kind, not the reindeer ones. I'm tired of antlers."

Caleb did a mock shocked expression. "But it's not even Christmas yet, bud."

The morning passed in slow motion. Ellie tried to eat breakfast and managed half a piece of toast. She showered, changed three times before settling on a blue sweater and jeans —professional enough for a video call but comfortable enough that she wouldn't feel constrained. She checked her email seventeen times even though Rebecca had told her the meeting wasn't until two.

At one-thirty, Caleb set up his laptop in his home office—a small room off the living room that served as his workspace when he needed to handle administrative tasks. The space was sparse but functional: a desk, a comfortable chair, good lighting, and—most importantly—a door that closed.

"I'll be right outside," he told her, adjusting the camera angle to frame her properly. "You won't be able to see me on screen, but I'll be here. You need anything—water, a break, moral support—you just say the word."

"What if I can't do this? What if I freeze up, or say something stupid, or—"

He cupped her face in both hands, forcing her to look at him. "Then you take a breath, and you try again. But you won't freeze. You're going to be brilliant and strong and you're going to get what you deserve. I believe in you, Ellie. Completely."

At 1:58, the video call link arrived. Ellie clicked it with shaking hands.

The screen divided into three squares. Rebecca on the left— professional, composed, her office background neat and orderly. Mark's lawyer on the right—a man in his fifties, expensive suit, the kind of polished aggression that came with high hourly rates. And in the bottom square, her own face looked back at her—pale, scared, but determined.

Mark wasn't on the call. Rebecca had insisted—no direct contact, all communication through lawyers. Ellie had never been more grateful for anything in her life.

"Good afternoon, everyone," Rebecca began, her voice crisp and professional. "Let's get started. My client is prepared to negotiate in good faith, but we need to establish some ground rules first."

Mark's lawyer—his name was Donald Pritchard, Ellie remembered—leaned forward. "Ms. Freeman, before we begin, I want to apologize for my client's behavior yesterday. It was inappropriate and won't happen again."

"Your client violated a restraining order," Rebecca said flatly. "That's not inappropriate. It's illegal. And the only reason we're not pursuing criminal charges right now is because we're giving you one chance to settle this fairly."

Pritchard's jaw tightened. "We're prepared to make a very generous offer."

"Then let's hear it."

For the next hour, they negotiated. The house—who kept it, what the buyout would be, how the equity would be split. The car that was technically in both their names. The joint bank account that Mark had emptied without telling her. The retirement accounts they'd started together.

Pritchard pushed for Mark to keep the house, to pay Ellie out at seventy cents on the dollar "because she abandoned the property."

Rebecca pushed back. "My client didn't abandon anything. She fled an abusive situation. If we want to discuss who damaged the property value, we can talk about the hole your client punched in the bedroom wall. I have photos. Should we submit those to the mediator?"

Pritchard's face darkened. "My client disputes the characterization of abuse—"

"Your client grabbed my client hard enough to leave bruises. He destroyed her property. He made her fear for her physical safety. I have medical records, police reports from the one time she called 911 before he convinced her to send them away, text messages from friends she confided in. Do you really want to argue this in front of a judge?"

The negotiation shifted.

Ellie kept her face neutral, her hands folded in her lap where the camera couldn't see them shaking. Every time Pritchard tried to paint Mark as reasonable, as the victim of Ellie's "instability," Rebecca countered with facts, with documentation, with the kind of devastating precision that came from knowing exactly how strong her position was.

"Let's discuss the pregnancy," Pritchard said finally.

Ellie's stomach dropped.

"My client wants it clearly stated that he has no parental rights or responsibilities. Ms. Freeman is free to raise the child as she sees fit, but my client will not be providing financial support or accepting any custodial arrangements."

"Documented and agreed," Rebecca said smoothly. "In exchange, my client wants it stated clearly that your client has no rights to visitation, custody, or any say in how the child is raised. He's terminating all parental rights permanently. No take-backs, no changes of heart down the road."

"Agreed."

"And in exchange for that termination—in exchange for my client taking on sole responsibility for this child—we're adjusting the property settlement. She keeps the house, your client pays her out for his half of the equity at full market value. Not seventy cents on the dollar. Full value. She also keeps the car, the joint savings that your client emptied gets replenished, and we're adding a ten-thousand-dollar settlement for emotional distress and the cost of relocating due to your client's harassment."

"That's ridiculous—"

"Is it? Because I have documentation of yesterday's restraining order violation. I have witnesses. I have a law enforcement officer's statement. I have months of harassing phone calls and emails. I have your client showing up at my client's workplace multiple times. I have enough to file charges that would result in jail time and a permanent record. So you can pay ten thousand dollars to make this go away quietly, or we can drag this through criminal court and civil court and every court in between. Your choice."

Pritchard muted his microphone. Ellie could see him on screen, clearly on another call—probably with Mark. The seconds stretched into minutes.

Finally he unmuted. "We'll agree to full market value on the house, the car, and replenishing the savings. Five thousand for emotional distress, not ten."

"Eight thousand. And your client signs a no-contact agreement that says if he violates the restraining order again, the settlement amount automatically increases by fifty thousand dollars. We'll call it a don't be a jerk tax."

Despite everything, Ellie almost laughed.

Pritchard looked like he'd swallowed a lemon. Another muted conversation with Mark. More minutes ticking past.

"Fine. Eight thousand. No-contact agreement with escalating penalties. We'll have documents drawn up by end of business tomorrow."

"Make it today," Rebecca said. "My client has been waiting long enough."

"Today is—"

"Today. Or we move forward with criminal charges. Your choice."

"Fine. Today. By six p.m."

"Pleasure doing business with you, Mr. Pritchard." Rebecca's smile was sharp enough to cut glass. "Ellie, you're free to go. I'll review the documents when they arrive and call you this evening."

The screen went dark.

Ellie sat frozen in the chair, unable to process what had just happened. The door opened and Caleb was there, pulling her out of the chair and into his arms.

"You did it," he said fiercely. "You won. Did you hear that? You won."

"I just—I sat here. Rebecca did everything."

"You showed up. You stayed calm. You didn't back down. That's everything." He pulled back to look at her, his eyes bright. "You're free, Ellie. By tonight, you'll have the documents that say you're free. Free from him, free from the marriage, free to build whatever life you want."

The reality of it hit her all at once, and she burst into tears—not sad tears, but the overwhelming kind that came from releasing months of tension and fear and carrying weight she could finally set down.

Caleb held her while she cried, one hand stroking her back, murmuring reassurances into her hair.

When she finally calmed, he walked her to the couch, settled her with blankets and tea, and called into the office to tell them he was taking the rest of the day off.

"You don't have to—" she started.

"I know. I want to." He sat beside her, pulling her feet into his lap. "Besides, Noah's going to be home in an hour, and he's going to want to celebrate. Kid has an uncanny sense for when good things happen."

"We can't tell him about the settlement. He's eight."

"We'll tell him something good happened and leave out the boring legal parts. He'll be satisfied with cake."

At three-thirty, Noah burst through the door with Mabel, who took one look at Ellie's tear-stained, smiling face and Caleb's protective positioning and clapped her hands together.

"Good news, I take it?"

"Very good news," Caleb confirmed.

"Well, praise Jesus and pass the sweet tea. I brought dinner—lasagna, garlic bread, and a chocolate cake that's probably illegal in some states. Figured you'd all be too tired to cook." She set the dishes on the counter with the efficiency of someone who'd been doing this for decades. "Now, I'm going to leave before I intrude on family time. But Ellie, honey—" she turned back, her eyes suspiciously bright "—your grandmother would be so proud. So very proud."

After she left, they ate dinner at the kitchen table—Noah chattering about his day, Tripod begging shamelessly for scraps, the evening news playing quietly in the background. Normal. Domestic. Everything Ellie had been afraid to hope for.

At six-fifteen, Rebecca called. "Documents are in your email. I've reviewed them—everything's exactly as we negotiated. You need to sign electronically, I'll file them tomorrow morning, and by end of next week you'll be officially divorced and free."

"Free," Ellie repeated, testing the word.

"Free. No more looking over your shoulder. No more waiting for him to show up. No more control. You're done."

After they hung up, Ellie signed the documents with shaking hands while Caleb read over her shoulder, making sure everything was correct.

When she clicked "submit" on the final signature, she felt something break loose in her chest—some tight, painful thing she'd been carrying for so long she'd forgotten what breathing without it felt like.

"It's done," she whispered.

"It's done," Caleb confirmed. He kissed her temple, soft and reverent. "You're free."

That night, after Noah was asleep and the house was quiet, Ellie stood in front of the Christmas tree, looking at the lights and the ornaments and the slightly crooked star that had watched over this family for so many years.

Caleb came up behind her, wrapped his arms around her waist, rested his chin on her shoulder.

"What are you thinking?" he asked quietly.

"That I spent so long running from the wrong thing that I almost missed running toward the right thing." She covered his hands with hers where they rested on her belly. "That I'm grateful my car went into that ditch. That I'm grateful you were the one who found me. That I'm grateful for every single thing that led me here, even the hard parts. Especially the hard parts."

"Me too," he said softly. "I didn't know how much I needed you until you were here. Didn't know how much Noah needed you. We were getting by, surviving. But with you—we're living again. Really living."

She turned in his arms, looked up at him in the soft glow of Christmas lights. "I love you. And I love Noah. And I love this life we're building. And I'm not running anymore. Not from this. Not from us."

"Good." His kiss was slow and deep and full of promise. "Because we're keeping you. Noah made a chart about it. It's legally binding now."

She laughed against his mouth. "Is that how it works?"

"In this house? Absolutely."

They stood there for a long time, swaying slightly to music only they could hear, wrapped in each other and the peace that came from finally being exactly where they belonged.

Outside, snow began to fall again—soft, steady, erasing every old track.

Inside, the Christmas tree lights blinked their steady pattern, and in the kitchen the chocolate cake sat half-eaten, and upstairs a little boy slept with a smile on his face because his prayers were being answered in ways he'd asked for and ways he hadn't even known to hope for.

And in the living room, two people who'd been broken in different ways stood whole in each other's arms, proof that sometimes the best families weren't born—they were chosen, built piece by piece, day by day, through courage and love and the willingness to stay even when running felt safer.

Free, Ellie thought again as Caleb led her upstairs, his hand warm and solid in hers. Finally, blessedly free. And choosing, with everything in her, to use that freedom to build something beautiful. Something lasting. Something that looked exactly like home.

Chapter 15

Friday morning dawned with the kind of stillness that felt like the world was holding its breath.

Ellie woke before Caleb this time, watched the winter sun paint gold across his sleeping face. In the soft morning light, the worry lines around his eyes smoothed out, making him look younger. Peaceful. She traced them with her eyes—the scar on his jaw from some long-ago accident, the silver starting to thread through his dark hair at the temples, the way his lashes cast shadows on his cheeks.

He'd given her so much in such a short time. Safety. Family. The space to remember who she was before Mark had convinced her she was someone smaller.

She pressed a hand to the curve of her stomach, whispering so quietly the words were more breath than sound. "You're going to love him, little one. He's already in love with you, even though we haven't met you yet. He's the kind of man who shows up. Who stays. Who means it when he says forever."

"Talking to our girl already?"

Ellie startled. Caleb's eyes were open now, watching her with that soft expression that made her heart do complicated things.

"Our girl?" she repeated, her pulse kicking up.

"Gut feeling. Noah's convinced it's a boy, but I think he's wrong." He reached out, rested his hand over hers on her belly. "Either way, this baby already has two people who'd walk through fire for them. Three if you count Noah, which you should because that kid's protective streak runs deep."

"Four if you count Tripod."

"Five if you count Mabel, though that's either a blessing or a curse depending on the day."

They lay there for a while longer, hands joined over the baby, watching sunlight creep across the room and turn everything golden.

"I have to tell you something," Caleb said finally, his voice careful. "And I don't want you to think I'm pushing, or assuming, or moving too fast. But I need to say it anyway."

Ellie's stomach tightened with apprehension. "Okay."

"I want you to stay. Not just until the baby comes. Not just until you figure out what's next. I want you to stay permanently. Here, with me and Noah. I want us to be a family—the real kind, the legal kind. I want to marry you, Ellie."

She stopped breathing entirely.

"I know it's fast," he continued, the words coming faster now like he'd been holding them back and couldn't anymore. "I know you just got out of one marriage and probably need time to heal. I know your divorce isn't even final yet. But I also know what I feel, and I know what I want, and I don't want to waste time pretending I don't."

"Caleb—"

"I'm not asking you to answer right now. I'm not even officially proposing yet—there's supposed to be a ring and a better speech and probably less bedhead." He ran a hand through his hair, making it stick up at odd angles. "I'm just saying—when you're ready, if you're ready—I'm here. I'm all in. I want forever with you."

Ellie's eyes burned with tears that seemed to be her permanent state lately. "You're really not worried? About the baby not being yours biologically? About taking on someone else's child?"

"Ellie." He shifted onto his elbow, looking down at her with fierce intensity. "I've been Noah's dad since the day Sarah died. Biology is just DNA. Parenting is showing up, day after day, even when it's hard. This baby—" he pressed his palm flat against her belly "—this baby is already mine in every way that matters. Already loved. Already wanted. The fact that someone else contributed half the genetics doesn't change a damn thing."

"What about Noah? Have you asked him how he feels about —"

"About having a baby sister or brother? He asked me last

night if we could paint the guest room yellow because 'babies like sunshine.' Kid's already planning nursery colors. He's in, Ellie. Completely."

She was crying in earnest now, the good kind of tears that came from being offered something she'd been afraid to even dream about. "I love you. So much it scares me sometimes."

"Yeah?" His smile was crooked, vulnerable. "Good. Because I love you more than is probably healthy for a man who's supposed to maintain professional composure."

She pulled him down and kissed him, deep and sure and full of promise for all the tomorrows they were building together.

Downstairs, Noah was already awake—they could hear him singing off-key to Christmas music and the sound of Tripod's tail thumping enthusiastically against the floor.

"Life awaits," Caleb said, stealing one more kiss before rolling out of bed. "Fair warning—Mabel texted me at six a.m. The festival committee has an emergency meeting at nine. Something about the gingerbread competition getting contentious."

"How does gingerbread get contentious?"

"This is Estrella Ridge. Everything gets contentious eventually. It's our town motto."

The emergency meeting turned out to be exactly as ridiculous as promised. Carol Jean Martinez and Linda Hoffsteader—a woman Ellie vaguely remembered from high school—were in a heated argument about whether using store-bought graham crackers in a gingerbread house counted as "homemade" or if everything had to be made from scratch.

"The rules say homemade gingerbread houses!" Linda insisted, her face red. "Not 'mostly homemade with some store-bought components!'"

"The rules say nothing about graham crackers!" Carol Jean shot back. "They're a structural element, not a decorative one!"

"Since when are walls not decorative?"

Pastor Mike looked like he was reconsidering his entire career in ministry.

Ellie stepped in before violence erupted over baked goods. "Two categories. One for completely from-scratch houses, one for mixed-media houses. We'll call it 'Traditional' and 'Innovative.' Judges will score them separately. Everyone gets to compete the way they want."

The room went silent.

"That's actually brilliant," Mabel said, looking impressed. "Why didn't we think of that?"

"Because you were all too busy arguing," Ellie said mildly. "Now, is there actual festival business to discuss, or was this entire meeting about crackers?"

There was actual business—finalizing the Christmas Eve schedule, coordinating volunteers for setup, making sure someone had ordered enough hot cocoa mix for the expected crowd. Ellie found herself taking notes, making suggestions, organizing logistics with the kind of practiced efficiency that came from years of project management in corporate settings.

She was good at this. Had forgotten she was good at this—at bringing order to chaos, at finding compromises that made everyone feel heard.

By the time the meeting ended two hours later, she had a color-coded schedule, a volunteer roster, and three new committees that somehow she'd ended up chairing.

"You're a natural," Mabel said as they filed out of the courthouse meeting room. "Ever think about running for town council? We could use someone with actual organizational skills instead of Bob Jensen, who mostly just shows up to meetings to complain about the library staying open past seven p.m."

"I'll think about it," Ellie heard herself say, surprising herself.

Because why not? Why not put down roots here? Why not build a life that included gingerbread politics and nativity donkeys and a town that adopted you whether you asked for it or not?

Walking back to Caleb's house—her house now, really, even if she hadn't officially moved her belongings from Nevada yet—Ellie felt something settle into place. Not perfectly, not without questions or uncertainties. But settled nonetheless.

She found Caleb in the kitchen making lunch while Noah did homework at the table. The scene was so domestic, so normal, so exactly what she'd always wanted but never thought she'd have.

"Hey," Caleb said, looking up from the sandwiches he was constructing. "How was the gingerbread summit?"

"Surprisingly productive. I'm now in charge of three committees and might be running for town council."

"That was fast. You've been here less than two weeks."

"Mabel works quickly."

"Mabel works terrifyingly." He slid a plate across to her—turkey and avocado, exactly how she liked it.

"Doc Martinez called. My test results came back perfect. Baby's healthy, I'm healthy, everything's exactly where it should be."

Noah looked up from his math worksheet. "When do we find out if it's a boy or girl?"

"A few more weeks," Ellie said, settling into the chair beside him. "Probably after Christmas."

"I hope it's a girl. Then we'd have even numbers. Two boys, two girls. That's fair."

"Wait—" Caleb held up a hand. "When did Ellie become a girl in the count? Last I checked, she was just staying here."

Noah looked at his father like he'd grown a second head. "Daddy. She's *staying* staying. Like, forever. I made a chart. It has projections."

"Of course you did."

"So that means she's family. Which means she counts in the numbers. Obviously."

Ellie felt her throat tighten with emotion. "Thank you, Noah. I'd be honored to count in the numbers."

"You're welcome. Now can someone help me with this word problem? It's about trains and I don't understand why trains are always going different speeds in math. In real life, trains just go train-speed."

The afternoon passed in the kind of easy domesticity that Ellie was still getting used to. Noah's homework turned into a discussion about whether trains could theoretically go fast enough to time travel. This led to an impromptu science lesson from Caleb about relativity that was mostly accurate and only slightly made up. Which led to Noah deciding he wanted to be a physicist when he grew up, or possibly a train conductor, or maybe both. As well as a part time sheriff, of course.

At four o'clock, Caleb's phone rang. He glanced at the screen, frowned slightly.

"Sheriff's department. I need to take this." He stepped into his office, closing the door.

He was gone for twenty minutes. When he emerged, his expression was carefully neutral—the cop face he wore when he was handling something serious.

"Everything okay?" Ellie asked.

"Yeah. Just—can we talk? Privately?"

Her stomach dropped. "Noah, can you take Tripod outside for a bit?"

"But it's cold—"

"Buddy," Caleb's voice was gentle but firm. "Outside. Ten minutes. Go."

Noah recognized that tone. He bundled up and took Tripod out without further protest, though he shot worried looks over his shoulder.

Once they were alone, Caleb sat beside Ellie on the couch, taking her hands. "That was the LAPD. Mark was arrested this morning."

Ellie's heart stopped. "What?"

"He showed up at your lawyer's office making threats. Apparently he was drunk, caused a scene, had to be physically removed by building security. Rebecca called the police, they arrested him."

"Oh my gosh."

"He's being held overnight, arraignment tomorrow morning. Rebecca wanted you to know. She said—" he paused, clearly choosing his words carefully "—she said this is good for your case. Shows a pattern of behavior, establishes that he's unstable and potentially dangerous. It's going to make the divorce proceedings even cleaner. He's basically gift-wrapped evidence that you were right to leave."

Ellie didn't know what she felt. Relief? Vindication? Fear that he'd blame her and come after her even harder once he was released?

"Hey." Caleb cupped her face, made her look at him. "This is good news, Ellie. I know it doesn't feel like it. But this is him destroying his own credibility. By the time he's out, your divorce will be finalized and he'll have a record. He can't hurt you anymore."

"What if he tries? What if he gets out and comes here and —"

"Then he deals with me. And the entire Estrella Ridge Sheriff's Department, which includes three deputies who are very protective of their town and especially protective of people I care about. And Pastor Mike, who's surprisingly intimidating when someone threatens his flock. And Mabel, who has connections I don't even want to know about."

Despite everything, Ellie laughed wetly. "I'm being protected by a small-town army."

"Damn right you are." He kissed her forehead. "Mark made his choices. He's living with the consequences. You don't have to feel guilty about that. You don't have to worry about him. You just have to focus on building your life—the one you deserve. The one that's waiting for you right here."

That evening, after Noah was in bed and they were curled together on the couch, Ellie's phone rang. Rebecca.

"Just wanted to update you," her lawyer said without preamble. "Mark's been charged with multiple counts—criminal trespass, public intoxication, and threatening behavior. His lawyer's trying to work out a plea deal. Part of that deal will include staying the heck away from you permanently. I expect we'll have the divorce finalized by end of next week, possibly sooner."

"So it's really over."

"It's really over. He's done, Ellie. Legally, financially, and by his own stupidity. You're free to live your life without looking over your shoulder."

After they hung up, Ellie sat in the quiet, processing.

Free. That word again. It still felt foreign, impossible, like trying on clothes in a size she didn't think would fit but discovering they were perfect.

"What are you thinking?" Caleb asked softly.

"That I spent so long being afraid of him, giving him so much power over my life. And in the end, he destroyed himself. I didn't have to do anything except survive and tell the truth."

"That's more than enough. Surviving takes courage. Telling the truth takes strength. You did both."

She turned to look at him in the firelight. "Earlier, you said you wanted to marry me. That you wanted forever."

His eyes sharpened, focused entirely on her. "I did."

"I'm not ready yet. I need time—time to be divorced, time to figure out who I am without being someone's wife, time to just breathe. But Caleb—" she took his hand, pressed it to her belly where the baby was doing gymnastics "—I want that too. When I'm ready. When enough time has passed that I know I'm choosing you for the right reasons, not just because you saved me. I want forever with you."

His smile was incandescent, lighting up his whole face. "Yeah?"

"Yeah. So if you're willing to wait—"

"I'd wait a lifetime for you, Ellie Freeman. But I don't think I'll have to." He kissed her softly. "Take all the time you need. I'm not going anywhere."

They sat like that for a long time, wrapped in each other and the warmth of the fire, planning a future that finally felt real and possible and theirs.

Outside, snow fell steadily, blanketing the world in white.

Chapter 16

Saturday arrived with Noah shaking Ellie awake at an hour that violated every unwritten law of weekend mornings.

"Ellie! Ellie, wake up!" His face materialized approximately three inches from hers, breath minty-fresh and eyes blazing with the kind of energy that suggested he'd been awake since before dawn, plotting. "It's sledding day! Mrs. Mabel said the whole town's going to Miller's Hill and there's gonna be hot chocolate and a bonfire and Dad said we can bring Tripod if we promise to watch him so he doesn't eat anyone's lunch!"

Ellie pried one eye open, then the other. Early morning light filtered through the curtains—pale winter sunshine that suggested it was barely past seven. Her body protested the interruption, the baby doing a lazy somersault that made her press a hand to her belly.

"Noah James." Caleb's voice came from the doorway, carrying that particular blend of resignation and barely-contained amusement that seemed to define single parenthood. He was already dressed, hair still damp from the shower, holding a coffee mug like a lifeline. "What did I say about waking people up before eight on weekends?"

"You said don't do it unless it's an emergency or something really, really exciting." Noah didn't sound remotely apologetic. His gap-toothed grin was pure mischief. "Sledding is really, really exciting, Daddy. It's basically an emergency of fun."

Caleb opened his mouth, clearly running through potential counter-arguments in his head, then apparently decided this was a battle not worth fighting. "Give Ellie ten minutes. Go feed Tripod and pack your snow stuff. The good mittens, not the ones with holes."

"But the holey ones are broken in—"

"Noah."

"Fine." Noah bounced off the bed with the elastic energy of

someone who'd probably been mentally preparing for this moment since he went to sleep. His footsteps thundered down the stairs, followed by Tripod's enthusiastic three-legged scramble and the sound of the dog food container being opened with more enthusiasm than skill.

Once the chaos had relocated to the kitchen, Caleb came into the room properly and sat on the edge of the bed. He ran a hand through his hair, making it stick up at odd angles. In the soft morning light, he looked younger—more like the boy she'd known in high school, before grief and responsibility had carved lines around his eyes.

"Sorry," he said, and he genuinely meant it. "I tried to redirect him to cartoons at six-thirty, but he was relentless. Kid woke up with a mission."

"It's okay." Ellie pushed herself upright, pillows bunching behind her back. One hand went automatically to her belly where the baby was settling back down, apparently deciding morning acrobatics could wait. "What exactly is sledding day?"

"Town tradition for the past few years. Not sure who started it or why. Happens every year between Christmas and New Year's, weather permitting." His mouth quirked in that crooked way that did unfair things to her pulse. "Everybody drags their kids—and themselves, let's be honest—to Miller's Hill and pretends they're only there for the children. Mabel brings enough hot chocolate to caffeinate a small army. There's usually a bonfire that someone feeds constantly like they're warding off Vikings. And someone always dislocates their pride, if not their shoulder."

Ellie raised an eyebrow. "Sounds dangerous for someone who's pregnant."

"You don't have to sled," he said quickly, and she could see the careful recalibration happening behind his eyes. "Most adults just stand around the fire, drinking cocoa and judging everyone else's technique. I thought it might be..." He hesitated, uncertainty flickering across his features like he wasn't entirely sure he had the right to ask what he was about to ask. "I thought it might be good for you. To see more of the town. Meet people outside of committee meetings and church. See what normal life looks like here now. No pressure though. If you hate it, I'll fake a sheriff's emergency and take you home. We'll pretend this never happened."

The subtext was clear: *I want you to like it here. I want you to see what we could have.*

Ellie felt something warm bloom in her chest, something that had nothing to do with blankets or morning sun.

"Okay," she said, surprising herself with how much she meant it. "Let's go sledding."

By nine a.m., half the town had descended on Miller's Hill like a friendly invasion force armed with sleds and thermoses.

The hill itself was less impressive than its name suggested—more of a glorified slope on the eastern edge of town that probably earned its designation through historical optimism rather than actual elevation. But it was perfect for sledding: steep enough to be exciting without being genuinely dangerous, long enough that the ride felt worthwhile, and ending in a wide flat area that prevented anyone from sledding directly into the pond at the bottom.

Children shrieked with joy as they flew down the slope on everything from fancy store-bought sleds with racing stripes to flattened cardboard boxes that probably violated multiple safety regulations but worked surprisingly well. Adults clustered near the bonfire with travel mugs clutched in gloved hands, pretending to supervise while laughing too loudly at every spectacular wipeout.

Mabel Hensley was already there, naturally—wearing a Santa hat that had seen better decades, wielding an industrial-sized ladle like a weapon, and dispensing hot chocolate with the authority of someone who'd appointed herself chief of winter beverages. Her station was set up near the fire, complete with a folding table covered in festive plastic tablecloth and enough paper cups to serve a small country.

"Noah, hon, bring that dog over here before he freezes his

remaining legs off!" she called the moment they arrived. Then she spotted Ellie and marched over with purpose. "And Ellie, honey—welcome! Look at you, practically glowing! That baby's treating you right."

Ellie felt heat climb her cheeks despite the cold. "We've established you have no concept of privacy, Mabel."

"Privacy is for people who don't live in towns where everyone shares casseroles and confessions," Mabel said cheerfully, pressing a steaming cup into Ellie's gloved hands. The liquid inside smelled like chocolate and cinnamon and melted marshmallows. "Drink this. You're growing a baby and feelings, and both require sugar."

Caleb made a strangled sound that might have been protest or laughter. "Mabel."

"What?" Mabel widened her eyes in theatrical innocence that fooled absolutely no one. "I didn't say anything she doesn't already know. Now, Sheriff, get yourself some cocoa before Tom Henderson drinks it all. Man has a hollow leg when it comes to hot beverages."

Noah came barreling up the slope then, cheeks already pink from cold and excitement, dragging a neon-green sled behind him like it was Excalibur. Tripod bounded beside him with his peculiar three-legged gait, leaving asymmetrical paw prints in the snow and looking delighted by literally everything—the cold, the people, the possibility of dropped food.

"Ellie!" Noah skidded to a stop in front of her, breathing hard. "You're gonna sit right there by the fire and watch me do the Big Hill Run. Daddy says I have to be safe but I told him safe is boring and then he said 'safe keeps you alive' and I said 'alive is important' and then we compromised that I can do it if I don't aim at old people or the Henderson twins."

"That seems like a reasonable compromise," Ellie said with appropriate solemnity.

Noah beamed like she'd endorsed a brilliant tactical strategy, then sprinted back toward the line of kids gathering at the top of the hill, sled bouncing behind him.

Ellie settled on one of the split-log benches near the fire, cradling her hot chocolate in both hands and letting warmth seep into fingers that were already going numb from the cold. The scene before her was something out of a postcard—or one of those overly earnest holiday movies her college roommate had loved. Families everywhere. Children tumbling through snow. Teenagers showing off for each other with increasingly risky sled maneuvers. Adults pretending they weren't having just as much fun as their kids.

How could she have ever despised this place? It was perfect.

Caleb stood behind her for a moment, and she felt rather than saw him doing what he always did—scanning the crowd with that cop's eye that never quite turned off. Checking for hazards, looking for problems, making sure everyone was safe. Then he sat beside her on the log, close enough that their shoulders brushed through layers of winter coat.

"You okay?" he asked quietly.

"I'm..." Ellie watched a group of teenagers launch themselves down the hill on what appeared to be a cafeteria tray, screaming like they'd just discovered immortality. "I'm okay. I forgot what this was like."

"Being cold and covered in snow?"

"Being..." She gestured vaguely at the chaos, the laughter, the way no one seemed too self-conscious or too cool to be completely ridiculous for an afternoon. "Being around people who remember you. People who show up. Who make space for you even when you haven't earned it."

Caleb didn't say *I told you so*. Didn't say *this could be yours forever if you stay*. He just nudged his shoulder against hers in that quiet way he had—offering support without demanding anything in return.

Noah's turn came moments later. He positioned himself at the top of the hill with the focus of an Olympic athlete, tongue poking out the corner of his mouth in concentration. Then he launched himself forward with a whoop that probably carried to the next county.

He rocketed down the slope, hair flying out from under his winter hat, arms spread wide like he was flying. He hit a small bump halfway down and went briefly airborne—just for a second, just enough to make Ellie's heart leap into her throat—before landing with a spray of powder. He made it to the flat area at the bottom, spun in a wild, uncontrolled circle, and toppled off his sled in an explosion of snow and joy.

Tripod charged after him like a three-legged ambulance, barking encouragement.

Ellie burst out laughing before she could stop herself. The sound felt strange coming out of her own throat—too bright, too unguarded—but it was real. Genuine. The kind of laughter she'd almost forgotten she could make.

When she looked over, Caleb was watching her instead of Noah. His expression was soft, unguarded in a way she rarely saw. Like her laughter mattered more than anything else happening on the hill.

"What?" she asked, suddenly self-conscious.

"Nothing." But his smile said everything. "Just... it's good to hear you laugh like that."

Later, after Noah had made approximately seventeen more runs and was showing no signs of slowing down, he came back to the bonfire panting and flushed.

"Daddy!" He grabbed Caleb's gloved hand with both of his. "You have to come down with me. Just once. Please? Everyone else's dads are sledding!"

Caleb glanced at Ellie with an expression that said *save me* and also *I'm absolutely going to do this.*

"I'm not sure—"

"Please?" Noah deployed his most devastating weapon: the gap-toothed pleading look that had probably gotten him out of countless timeouts. "I'll do all my homework without complaining for a whole week."

"That's a blatant lie and we both know it," Caleb said, but he was already standing up, dusting snow off his jeans.

"It's a Christmas season promise," Noah amended. "Those

are different. They count extra."

Caleb looked at Ellie one more time, and she could see he was asking permission for something—though whether it was permission to act like a kid for ten minutes or permission to show her this side of himself, she wasn't sure.

"Go," she said, smiling. "Show him how it's done."

What followed was possibly the least graceful sledding run in Miller's Hill history.

Caleb folded his tall frame onto Noah's neon-green sled with all the elegance of a giraffe attempting yoga. Noah wedged himself in front, practically vibrating with excitement. They pushed off, Caleb trying desperately to maintain some semblance of dignity and failing spectacularly.

"FASTER!" Noah shrieked like he was commanding a starship.

"We're literally in free fall, I can't make gravity work harder!" Caleb shouted back.

They hit the same bump Noah had caught earlier. This time, both of them went airborne. For a glorious, ridiculous second, they hung suspended—father and son, silhouetted against white snow and blue sky.

Then they crashed in a tangle of limbs and laughter and sled, tumbling the last twenty feet in a spray of powder. They came to rest in a heap at the bottom, Caleb flat on his back, Noah sprawled across him, both of them laughing so hard they could barely breathe.

Tripod arrived moments later, barking frantically and trying to lick everyone's face at once, apparently convinced he was needed for first aid.

Ellie stood near the fire, one hand pressed over her mouth, laughing until tears froze on her cheeks.

Mabel appeared at her elbow, voice low and satisfied. "That," she said, nodding toward the scene at the bottom of the hill where Caleb was now being used as a sled by his son, "is what healing looks like. Don't fight it, honey."

Ellie wanted to argue. Wanted to insist she wasn't healed yet

—wasn't ready, wasn't sure, wasn't anything except terrified of hoping too hard and losing everything again.

But Noah's laughter carried up the hill, pure and uncomplicated, and Caleb was grinning like he'd forgotten how to do anything else. And something in Ellie's chest—something that had been clenched tight for so long she'd forgotten what it felt like to be loose—finally began to unwind.

By the time the sun started its descent and the cold sharpened from pleasant to biting, they headed home. Noah was practically unconscious on Caleb's back, making sleepy observations about aerodynamics that were mostly nonsense. Tripod trotted behind, leaving his signature three-legged prints and looking enormously pleased with himself for reasons that remained mysterious.

At the front door, Noah stirred enough to mumble into Caleb's coat, "This was the best day. Almost as good as Christmas Eve is gonna be."

Ellie paused, one hand on the doorframe. "Christmas Eve?"

Noah's eyes snapped open like someone had pulled an alarm. Suddenly he was very, very awake. "The live nativity! With the real animals! And the children's choir! And the whole town comes and there's candles and singing and Kevin the donkey! And Mrs. Mabel says you're gonna be part of it!"

Caleb shot Ellie a look over Noah's head that clearly said *I tried to prevent this conversation, but she moves in mysterious and unstoppable ways.*

Ellie stared between father and son. "I'm going to be in the nativity?"

Noah nodded so vigorously his whole body moved. "Yes! Mrs. Mabel measured you last week when you weren't paying attention. She does that. She's sneaky. That means it's official."

"Measured me for what, exactly?"

"The costume!" Noah said this like it should be obvious. "You're gonna be so pretty!"

Ellie's stomach dropped. "I'm sorry, what?"

Caleb shifted Noah's weight on his back and unlocked the

door. "We'll discuss this inside. Where it's warm. And where I have plausible deniability if you decide to murder Mabel."

"I'm seriously considering it," Ellie muttered, following them in.

But despite everything—despite the surprise conscription into small-town theater, despite her instinct to run from anything that put her on display—a small, traitorous part of her was already imagining what it might feel like.

To stand up there on Christmas Eve. To be part of something instead of watching from the edges. To let this town claim her the way it had been trying to since the moment her car went into that ditch.

Outside, the town lights began flickering on one by one, warm gold against the deepening blue of dusk. Snow started falling again—soft, steady, the kind that muffled sound and made everything feel held.

And for the first time since she'd driven back into Estrella Ridge, Ellie didn't feel like she was just passing through.

She felt like she might actually be arriving.

Chapter 17

The week that followed moved with a strange kind of inevitability, like Estrella Ridge had decided what Ellie needed before she'd figured it out herself and was now gently but firmly dragging her toward it.

Monday brought a rehearsal at the church. Tuesday brought a committee meeting that somehow turned into a potluck. Wednesday brought Carol Jean Martinez to the door with a box of maternity clothes "that my daughter-in-law never wore, practically brand new, and you'd be doing me a favor taking them off my hands."

The parade of kindness was relentless. Neighbors stopped by with extras they "just happened to have"—cookies from batches that were "too big," hand-knitted baby blankets from someone's aunt who'd "made too many," a bassinet that Tom Henderson swore he'd been meaning to donate for years.

Every gift came with the same casual dismissal, the same implication that Ellie was doing them a favor by accepting. No one wanted credit. No one wanted thanks. They just wanted her to have what she needed.

It was overwhelming. It was uncomfortable. It was the most loved Ellie had felt in years.

She tried to tell herself she was only staying because the roads had been bad and Ruth's house was still a frozen disaster and her car was still in Ron's shop waiting for parts that were apparently being shipped from the automotive equivalent of outer space.

Practical reasons. Temporary reasons. Exit strategies.

But the truth was becoming harder to ignore: the longer she stayed, the less the word *temporary* fit in her mouth.

Wednesday afternoon found her at the church with Pastor Mike, ostensibly practicing the nativity narration but mostly trying not to laugh every time Kevin the donkey decided to provide live commentary.

The sanctuary smelled like furniture polish and candlewax and decades of potluck dinners. Winter light streamed through the stained-glass windows, throwing colored patterns across the wooden floor—ruby reds and sapphire blues that moved as clouds passed overhead.

Pastor Mike stood near the makeshift stable, clipboard in hand, looking like a man who'd made peace with chaos but wasn't entirely happy about it.

"So you'll stand here," he said, gesturing to a spot stage-left of the manger scene. "Read from Luke, chapter two. Pause for the children's choir. Try not to laugh when Kevin inevitably does something ridiculous."

As if on cue, Kevin—who was supposed to be standing peacefully beside the manger—stretched his neck forward and grabbed a mouthful of straw from the roof.

"Kevin," Pastor Mike said wearily. "That is structural."

Kevin chewed thoughtfully, unrepentant.

Ellie pressed a hand to her mouth, shoulders shaking with suppressed laughter.

"He has opinions," she managed.

"He has *many* opinions," Pastor Mike corrected. "And he shares them frequently and at high volume. Last year he brayed during the Lord's Prayer. People thought it was scripted. We got letters."

Ellie scratched behind Kevin's ears, and the donkey leaned into her hand with a contented sigh. "He just wants artistic input."

"What he wants is to be the star of the show." Pastor Mike adjusted his glasses and made a note on his clipboard. "Which, theologically speaking, is deeply problematic but also completely inevitable."

"Is it though?" smiled Ellie. "What about Balaam's donkey?"

"Good point!" Pastor Mike pushed up his glasses. "I can't argue with you there!"

The church door banged open and Mabel swept in with the

force of a woman on a mission from God—or at least from the Estrella Ridge Christmas Festival Committee, which sometimes amounted to the same thing.

"Excellent news!" she announced, as if she'd been personally responsible for brokering world peace. "We're adding an angel!"

Pastor Mike's pen froze mid-note. "We already have angels. The children's choir is dressed as—"

"No, no, no." Mabel waved this away like she was clearing smoke. "We need *one* angel. One big, visible, glorious angel that people can see from the street. Something dramatic. Something people will photograph and put on Facebook. Something that says 'this is a production, not just kids in bathrobes.'"

Ellie's stomach began a slow descent toward her feet.

Pastor Mike's eyebrows climbed toward his hairline. "Mabel, we've been over this. The budget—"

"The costume is already made," Mabel said triumphantly. "I sewed it myself. Measured and everything."

Ellie's voice came out smaller than she intended. "Mabel—"

Mabel turned to her with the expression of someone revealing a wonderful surprise. "Ellie will do it!"

Pastor Mike blinked. "Ellie is already narrating."

"She can narrate *and* be an angel," Mabel said as if this were the most logical thing in the world. "Stand off to the side. Look angelic. Read in that lovely city voice she has. It'll be beautiful. Spiritual. People will cry."

"I am pregnant," Ellie said, somewhat desperately.

"Exactly!" Mabel clasped her hands together like Ellie had just proven her point. "You already have that Madonna glow. We just add wings. Some gold trim. Maybe a halo. You'll be stunning."

The door opened again and Caleb walked in, presumably to collect Noah from choir practice. He took one look at the scene—Ellie's panicked expression, Pastor Mike's resignation, Mabel's unholy glee—and his cop instincts clearly told him he'd just walked into something.

"What's happening?" he asked carefully, like a man entering a room where someone might be holding scissors.

"Ellie's our Christmas angel!" Mabel beamed.

Caleb's gaze flicked to Ellie. Ellie's expression screamed *HELP ME.*

He cleared his throat diplomatically. "Mabel, I'm not sure that's—"

"She's already measured," Mabel steamrolled right over him. "And I told the festival committee. And the costume is finished. And honestly, Sheriff, it's Christmas Eve. Sometimes you have to let tradition happen."

Caleb looked like a man watching his best arguments evaporate before they could fully form.

Noah, who had been lurking in the hallway waiting for his father, burst into the sanctuary with the timing of someone who'd been eavesdropping.

"ELLIE'S GONNA BE AN ANGEL?" His face lit up like someone had just told him Christmas was coming early. "That means you're like an actual angel! From the Bible! But also alive! Which is even better because you can have cookies!"

"Noah—" Caleb started.

But Noah had already clasped his hands together in the universal gesture of a child about to deploy maximum emotional manipulation. "Please, Ellie. *Please* be the angel."

Ellie looked at Noah's shining face. At Mabel's determined expression. At Pastor Mike's weary but hopeful look that suggested he'd given up on controlling anything related to this production weeks ago.

She should say no. She'd spent years learning to set boundaries, learning that "no" was a complete sentence, learning that she didn't have to make herself uncomfortable just to make other people happy.

But Noah was looking at her like she'd hung the moon. And Mabel had apparently sewn an entire costume on the assumption that Ellie would say yes. And Pastor Mike needed help wrangling Kevin and a dozen eight-year-olds in bathrobes and the structural integrity of a cardboard stable.

More than that: a part of Ellie—the part that remembered being a child at Christmas Eve services, the part that remembered Grandma Ruth humming carols while she braided Ellie's hair, the part that was tired of being afraid—actually *wanted* to say yes.

"Fine," she heard herself say, the word coming out before her anxiety could stop it. She pointed at Mabel like she was signing a binding contract. "But if I fall off a platform in front of the entire town, you're the one catching me."

Mabel's smile could have powered the entire light display. "Caleb can catch you. He's taller."

Caleb made a sound that might have been a laugh or a prayer for patience.

The rehearsals intensified after that.

Thursday afternoon: practicing her stance and learning not to wobble when the wings shifted. Friday morning: running through the full program three times while Kevin tried to eat someone's mittens. Saturday: a final dress rehearsal where the children's choir forgot half their lyrics and one of the sheep escaped and had to be retrieved from the church kitchen.

Through it all, Caleb hovered at the edges—not hovering in the smothering way Mark used to hover, watching for mistakes so he could correct them later. Caleb's presence was different. Steadying. He was simply *there*, ready if she needed him, but trusting her to handle things on her own.

She caught him watching her sometimes with an expression she couldn't quite name—something between pride and wonder, like he was still half-convinced she might vanish if he blinked too hard.

Thursday night, after Noah had finally crashed from exhaustion and sugar, Ellie found Caleb in the kitchen making hot chocolate with the focused intensity of a man attempting to solve a complex equation.

"You're making it wrong," she said from the doorway.

He glanced over his shoulder, feigning offense. "Excuse you. I am a certified expert in hot chocolate preparation."

"You're using water."

"That's how Noah likes it."

Ellie crossed to the counter and took the wooden spoon from his hand, their fingers brushing in the transfer. "That's because Noah has the refined palate of a raccoon who got into the garbage."

Caleb's mouth twitched. "Are you comparing my son to a raccoon?"

"I'm saying your son would eat glitter if someone told him it was festive seasoning."

He laughed—a real laugh, the kind that made his shoulders shake and his eyes crinkle at the corners. The sound filled the kitchen with warmth that had nothing to do with the stove.

Ellie added milk to the pot, stirring slowly while Caleb stood beside her. They worked in comfortable silence, hands occasionally brushing as he reached for mugs or she reached for the cocoa tin.

Finally, voice pitched low enough that it felt private even in the empty kitchen, Caleb said, "You don't have to do the angel thing if you change your mind."

Ellie kept stirring, watching chocolate melt into milk. "I already changed my mind."

He turned to look at her fully. "About what?"

She paused, spoon hovering.

About this town. About whether small means simple. About what it means to be known. About running away from love because I was afraid of losing myself in it.

But she wasn't ready to say all that out loud yet. Some truths needed time to settle into bones before they could be spoken without trembling.

"About hiding," she said instead.

Caleb's expression gentled into something that looked dangerously close to hope. "Good."

Ellie set down the spoon and surprised them both by stepping closer, close enough to rest her forehead briefly against his chest —just for a moment, just long enough to feel the steady thump of his heart and remember what safe felt like.

His hand came up slowly, carefully, like he was afraid sudden movement might spook her. It settled at the back of her head, warm and solid, a quiet benediction that asked for nothing and offered everything.

"I'm proud of you," he murmured into her hair.

Ellie squeezed her eyes shut. "Don't."

"I'm going to," he said, gentle but immovable. "Because you deserve to hear it. You deserve to know you're doing something brave."

She wanted to argue. Wanted to insist that agreeing to wear wings and read Scripture wasn't brave, it was just... showing up. Being part of something. Saying yes instead of no.

But maybe that was exactly what brave looked like sometimes. Not grand gestures or dramatic stands, but small daily choices to stay instead of run.

"Thank you," she whispered against his shirt.

"For what?"

"For making me think I could do this."

His arms came around her then, carefully, giving her space to pull away if she needed to. When she didn't, he held her properly—not crushing, not claiming, just holding. Like she was something precious that had been missing and was finally, impossibly, home.

They stood like that while the hot chocolate simmered and snow began falling outside the window and somewhere upstairs Noah talked in his sleep about dinosaurs and Christmas cookies.

And Ellie let herself be held without flinching, without planning her escape, without waiting for the moment it would all fall apart.

For the first time in longer than she could remember, she let herself just be.

Chapter 18 — Christmas Eve

Christmas Eve arrived the way Christmas Eve always arrived in Estrella Ridge: with determination, excessive enthusiasm, and the kind of aggressive cheerfulness that couldn't be stopped by anything short of a natural disaster.

Ellie woke to Noah's voice echoing through the house like a tornado siren made of pure joy.

"IT'S THE DAY! IT'S CHRISTMAS EVE! It's the second best day before the very best day of the whole entire year!"

Tripod barked in emphatic agreement, his tail thumping against furniture hard enough to rattle picture frames. Somewhere below, Caleb made a sound that was half groan, half prayer for patience, followed by the blessed sound of the coffee maker beginning its morning ritual.

Ellie lay still for a moment, staring at the ceiling of what had become her room, listening to the beautiful chaos of this house that had somehow become hers without her quite noticing when the transition happened.

She should feel panicked. Overwhelmed. The old instinct to run was always there, coiled and ready like a muscle memory from years of survival.

Instead, she felt... steady. Not calm like nothing could go wrong, but calm like she could handle it if it did. Calm like she'd finally stopped waiting for permission to be here.

She swung her legs out of bed and padded to the mirror. Her reflection looked more like herself these days—less hollow, less braced for impact. The baby bump was undeniable now, rounding out the front of her sweater no matter how she tried to angle herself. She smoothed a hand over it and felt an answering flutter, like the baby was also waking up and checking the schedule.

"Okay," she murmured to her reflection and the tiny life beneath her ribs. "We're doing this."

Downstairs, Noah had somehow managed to dress himself in his shepherd costume without adult supervision, which meant his brown robe was on backwards, his rope belt was tied in a knot that could only be undone with scissors or divine intervention, and his shepherd's headdress sat at a confident diagonal that suggested either creative interpretation or structural failure.

He saw Ellie descending the stairs and froze mid-cereal-bite, eyes shining with the weight of cosmic importance.

"Today," he announced with the gravity of someone delivering a papal decree, "is the angel day."

Caleb emerged from the kitchen carrying two mugs—coffee for himself, something that smelled suspiciously like hot chocolate with extra marshmallows for her. He took one look at Noah's costume situation and visibly recalibrated his morning plans.

"Buddy," he said carefully, like a man approaching an unexploded ordinance, "your robe is—"

"It's fashion," Noah interrupted with the confidence of someone who'd already prepared his defense. "You wouldn't understand, being so old."

Ellie laughed. "He has a point. You *are* pretty old."

Caleb shot her a look. "Watch it. You're only three months younger than me."

Caleb's gaze slid back to Ellie over Noah's head. There was humor there, but something else too—something warmer and more permanent that made her pulse do complicated things.

"Coffee," he said, offering her the mug that definitely wasn't coffee. Their fingers brushed in the transfer, a spark of contact that felt deliberate. "For your patience. You're going to need it today."

"Thank you," she said, and meant more than the cocoa.

Mabel arrived at ten o'clock sharp with a garment bag the size of a body bag and the unstoppable energy of someone who believed sleep was optional during the month of December and possibly also a sign of weak character.

"All right, angel!" She swept into the living room like she owned the place, which in some cosmic sense she might. The woman had a key to half the houses in town and a proprietary interest in everyone's business. "Time to transform you into celestial glory."

Ellie eyed the garment bag with the kind of suspicion usually reserved for ticking packages. "Mabel—"

"No backing out," Mabel said briskly, already heading for the stairs like a general leading troops into battle. "I have measured you. I have sewn with these two hands. I have prayed over every seam. Also I told everyone in town you were doing this, so backing out now would basically constitute a scandal. Scandals are bad for property values. Come along."

Caleb took a slow, deliberate sip of his coffee—the posture of a man who had learned through hard experience that self-preservation sometimes meant staying very, very still while chaos moved around him.

"IS THERE A HALO?" Noah shouted after them, bouncing on his toes.

"There's a halo!" Mabel called back without breaking stride. "And wings! Big ones!"

Ellie closed her eyes briefly and sent up a prayer that was equal parts plea for strength and apology for whatever was about to happen. "Of course there are."

Upstairs in the guest bathroom, Mabel transformed into something between a stage mother and a military general, fussing over Ellie with the focused intensity of someone preparing a bride for a royal wedding rather than a small-town nativity with a donkey who had opinions about Scripture.

The costume was... a lot.

White robe that flowed all the way to the floor in soft folds. Gold sash that wrapped around her waist—or tried to, before making necessary accommodations for the baby bump. Wings made of wire frames and white feathers that were larger than her torso and attached with what appeared to be industrial-strength elastic and possibly prayer. A halo headband that perched precariously on her hair, already listing slightly to the left like it had doubts about its structural integrity.

Ellie stared at herself in the mirror, trying to decide if she looked more like a heavenly messenger or a woman who had lost a very elaborate bet.

She looked like a nativity-themed disco ball.

"Perfect," Mabel declared, stepping back to admire her handiwork with the satisfaction of an artist completing a masterpiece. "You're radiant. Ruth would cry."

Ellie eyed her reflection again, watching the wings wobble when she breathed. "Ruth would laugh herself sick."

"She would love it," Mabel corrected firmly. "You look festive. And tall. Which is important for angels. People like a tall angel. It gives the role authority."

Ellie lifted one wing experimentally. It wobbled alarmingly, threatening to take out the shower curtain.

"Great," she muttered. "Even my wings are uncertain about this decision."

Mabel patted her arm, softening just a fraction. Her eyes were suspiciously bright behind her rhinestone-studded glasses. "Honey, it's Christmas Eve. Nobody's looking for perfection. They're looking for a story. And you—" her gaze flicked to Ellie's belly, then back to her face "—you are a story. Whether you like it or not."

Ellie's throat tightened at that, so she just nodded and let Mabel fix the halo one more time, even though they both knew it wouldn't stay.

By the time dusk arrived, the town square looked like somebody had tried to outdo a Hallmark set designer and won.

Lights wrapped every tree trunk in spirals of white and gold. Lanterns lined the walkways, their flames protected by glass chimneys that made them look like they'd been borrowed from a Dickens novel. The giant Christmas tree stood in the center of the square, its star on top catching the last rays of sunlight and throwing them back in defiant brilliance.

The gazebo had been wrapped in fresh pine garland and red

velvet bows that were probably a fire hazard but looked stunning. A bonfire crackled near the hot cocoa tables, where people clustered with steaming cups and rosy cheeks, their laughter carrying across the square in waves.

The live nativity was set up on a raised platform near the church steps—hay bales arranged just so, a stable frame that looked surprisingly sturdy for something built by volunteers, Mary and Joseph waiting in their borrowed robes and looking nervous. The children's choir stood in formation wearing their angel costumes, wings made from coat hangers and tinsel that sparkled under the lights.

Pastor Mike stood to the side doing last-minute damage control with a clipboard and the expression of a man who had made peace with chaos but wasn't entirely happy about it.

Kevin the donkey brayed at a particularly dramatic moment in the sound check, and Pastor Mike sighed like this was his thirteenth reason for going gray before fifty.

Ellie stood off to the side in her ridiculous costume, gripping the microphone with both hands, wings rustling every time she moved or breathed or existed. She tried to breathe normally. Tried to pretend she wasn't about to read Scripture in front of most of the town while dressed like a seasonal bird.

Her hands were shaking. The baby was doing gymnastics. Her halo was slipping again.

Caleb stepped up behind her.

Not in a way that crowded her or made her feel trapped. In a way that anchored. His presence was solid and steady, like a wall you could lean against when the wind got too strong.

His hand rested lightly at the small of her back, warm through the layers of costume. Not possessive. Just... there.

"You're okay," he murmured close enough that only she could hear, his breath warm against her ear. "Breathe. They're not here to judge. They're here because they love this town and they love Christmas and half of them are just hoping Kevin does something hilarious. You're going to be perfect."

Ellie let out a shaky laugh that was half panic, half genuine amusement. "If I fall off this platform in front of everyone, I'm suing Mabel for emotional damages."

"I'll catch you," he said, like it was nothing. Like it was obvious. Like there was never any question that he'd be there when she fell.

The words hit her harder than they should have, settling somewhere deep in her chest where broken things had started healing.

Then Pastor Mike nodded to her, his smile gentle and encouraging.

Ellie lifted the microphone. Her voice carried out over the crowd, amplified and strange to her own ears. The words were familiar—Luke chapter two, verses she'd heard a thousand times as a kid and avoided for years as an adult—but tonight they landed differently. Less like obligation, more like something old and steady that hadn't gone anywhere just because she'd stopped paying attention.

"And it came to pass in those days, that there went out a decree from Caesar Augustus..."

The crowd was silent, attentive. Children fidgeted but parents held them still. Teenagers actually put down their phones. Old Mrs. Patterson had her good camera out, flash ready.

A gust of wind caught one of Ellie's wings halfway through the reading and lifted it like a sail trying to catch a breeze.

Ellie wobbled, grabbing for balance.

The crowd gasped collectively, a hundred people holding their breath.

Noah, standing in the front row in his backward shepherd's robe, whispered loudly enough to be heard in the next county, "DON'T FALL, ELLIE! ANGELS ARE SUPPOSED TO BE GRACEFUL!"

Ellie shot him a look that promised consequences later. The crowd laughed—warm, affectionate laughter that loosened the knot of tension in her chest. Someone actually clapped like she'd done it on purpose.

She finished the reading, managing not to fall or lose any

major costume pieces in the process. The children's choir sang "Silent Night" with the earnest, off-key sincerity that made grown adults reach for tissues. The tree lights shimmered against the darkening sky. Snow started coming down harder, thick flakes drifting through the beams of light like someone was shaking a giant snow globe.

When it ended, the crowd began drifting toward the cocoa tables and the bonfire, voices raised in conversation and laughter.

Ellie exhaled hard and turned to escape—wings first— toward the church where she could peel off this costume before she accidentally knocked over a small child.

But then she noticed something odd.

People weren't leaving. Not really. They were... gathering. Phones came out. Whispers moved through the crowd like wind through wheat. Heads turned toward the Christmas tree. Bodies shifted, making space.

A cleared area opened up near the base of the tree, right in the center of everything, like the town itself was making room for something planned.

Ellie slowed, frowning. "What are they—"

Caleb's hand found hers, fingers threading through hers with gentle certainty. She looked at him. He was still, but not stiff. Focused. Nervous in a way she'd never seen him nervous before. Like he'd made a decision that terrified him but he was committed to seeing it through.

"Noah," Caleb called, his voice carrying.

Noah appeared instantly like he'd been waiting for his cue, practically vibrating with barely contained excitement. "YES?"

"Bring Tripod."

Noah's grin split his face so wide it looked painful. He snagged Tripod's leash and trotted toward the center of the square like a tiny stage manager who'd been rehearsing this moment for weeks. The dog hopped along on three legs looking delighted to be included in whatever was happening.

Ellie's heart started beating too fast, her pulse loud in her ears.

Caleb guided her forward—through the crowd, through the ring of watching faces and glowing lights and falling snow. She was acutely aware of her ridiculous wings, her slipping halo, the absurdity of her outfit. She was aware of the baby shifting inside her, as if also paying attention to whatever was about to happen.

They reached the cleared space at the tree. Caleb stopped and turned to face her. All around them, Estrella Ridge held its breath. The only sounds were the crackling of the bonfire and the soft whisper of snow falling.

Ellie's palms went damp inside her gloves. "Caleb... what's happening?"

His mouth twitched, like he might have tried to make a joke and couldn't find one good enough for this moment.

"I'm not good at speeches," he said, his voice carrying just far enough.

Somebody in the crowd—probably Tom Henderson—called out, "THANK GOODNESS," and got immediately shushed by multiple people.

Ellie let out a breath that was half laugh, half pure panic.

Caleb's gaze stayed on her, steady and honest and more vulnerable than she'd ever seen him.

"I didn't plan this the way Mabel plans things," he said, and a few people laughed softly because everyone knew that kind of planning was impossible for mere mortals. "But I couldn't let tonight go by without saying what I need to say."

He swallowed once, and she could see it—the fear that he was doing this wrong, that he was pushing too hard, that he might lose her.

"I know your life got turned upside down," Caleb said, his voice low but carrying in the winter quiet. "I know you didn't come back here because you wanted to. You came back because you were out of options and running out of road."

Ellie's throat tightened.

"And I know you've been telling yourself you're temporary," he continued, words coming steadier now like he'd been holding them back too long and they'd built up pressure. "That you're just here until the road clears, until the house gets fixed, until the car is repaired. Until you can leave without feeling like you're running."

Snow landed on his shoulders, melted in his hair. He didn't seem to notice.

"But the thing is," he said, "you're not the only one who's been changing these past weeks."

Her breath hitched.

Caleb took both her hands fully now, holding them between his own, grounding her.

"I don't want to be a stop on your way to somewhere else," he said quietly. "I don't want one good season with you and then a goodbye I have to pretend I'm fine with. I want... a life. With you."

The crowd was completely silent now—no jokes, no commentary, just the crackle of the fire and the soft fall of snow and two hundred people bearing witness to something sacred.

Caleb's voice roughened a fraction.

"I want you here when Noah wakes up at three in the morning convinced he heard Santa on the roof. I want you here when the baby's teething and we're both exhausted and arguing over whose turn it is to check the diaper. I want you here when it's not magical or special. When it's just Tuesday and we're doing laundry and figuring out what's for dinner. I want all of it. Every ordinary, extraordinary day."

Ellie blinked hard. Tears blurred the lights into soft halos around everything.

Caleb drew a breath, then let it out slowly.

And then he dropped to one knee in the snow beneath the town's Christmas tree, right in the center of everything, in front of everyone who mattered.

A sound went through the crowd—a collective gasp, a wave of recognition and joy.

Ellie's hand flew to her mouth. Her wings rustled and her halo finally gave up and slipped sideways but she didn't care, couldn't care about anything except Caleb kneeling in the snow looking up at her like she was the answer to every prayer he'd been afraid to speak out loud.

He opened a small velvet box. The ring inside caught the light from the Christmas tree, glinting bright against the night and the snow.

"Ellie Freeman," he said, his voice steady despite the emotion roughening the edges, "will you marry me? Will you stay here and build a life with me and Noah? Will you let us be your family?"

For a second that stretched into eternity, Ellie couldn't move.

She stood there in her ridiculous angel costume with her slipping halo and her oversized wings, snow collecting on her shoulders, the whole town watching, the baby doing somersaults inside her, her heart too full and too terrified and too alive all at once.

This was what she'd been running from for so long. Not this town. Not these people. Not even the memories.

The possibility of being loved well. The possibility of staying and not losing herself. The possibility that broken things could be made whole without erasing the cracks.

Her voice came out as a whisper at first, barely audible even to herself.

"Yes."

Caleb's eyes flashed with something fierce and grateful and overwhelmed.

Then Ellie laughed through her tears and said it louder, because the town deserved to hear it and because she deserved to say it out loud without fear.

"Yes. Yes, I'll marry you."

The square erupted.

Cheers exploded into the night like fireworks made of sound. Someone started chanting "SHE SAID YES" and it caught like wildfire, spreading through the crowd. Mrs. Patterson's camera flash went off three times in rapid succession, probably blinding someone. Mabel made a noise that was half sob, half victory cry, and several people near her had to steady her before she fell over from excitement.

Caleb stood, hands shaking as he slid the ring onto her finger.

It fit perfectly.

Of course it fit.

Ellie sobbed once, then laughed, then reached for him and kissed him like she didn't care who saw, like she wasn't thinking about anything except the fact that this was real and he was real and she was choosing this, choosing him, choosing to stay.

When they broke apart—both breathing hard, both grinning like idiots—Noah tackled them with the force of a small, enthusiastic missile.

"I KNEW IT!" he shrieked, wrapping his arms around both their legs. "I TOTALLY KNEW IT! DADDY YOU DID THE SPEECH PERFECT! ELLIE YOU SAID YES! WE'RE A REAL FAMILY NOW!"

Caleb's voice went thick with emotion. He ruffled Noah's hair with one hand while keeping the other arm around Ellie. "We already were a real family, bud."

"Yeah," Noah insisted, eyes shining with unshed tears of joy. "But now it's official. Now we can tell people. Now Tripod can wear a bow tie at the wedding because I googled it and dogs definitely can wear bow ties and look distinguished."

Tripod barked once, as if endorsing this entire plan.

The crowd pressed in then—a wave of hugs and congratulations and laughter and love that threatened to sweep them all away. Pastor Mike appeared to offer a warm handshake and an even warmer smile, his eyes suspiciously bright. Tom Henderson clapped Caleb on the back hard enough to make him stumble. Carol Jean Martinez hugged Ellie so tight her wings bent.

Mabel pushed through the crowd with the determination of a woman on a mission, grabbed Ellie by the shoulders, and pulled her into a hug that felt like it was trying to fuse their ribcages together.

"About time," she whispered fiercely into Ellie's ear. "Your grandmother is up there throwing a party right now. I can feel it. She knew. She always knew you'd come home when you were ready."

Ellie laughed through fresh tears. "That sounds exactly like her."

As the crowd slowly drifted back toward the cocoa and the bonfire and their own warm houses, as the spontaneous celebration dissolved into the comfortable chaos of small-town Christmas Eve, Caleb leaned close enough that only Ellie could hear.

"Come on," he murmured, his breath warm against her cold cheek. "Let's go home."

Home.

The word settled over Ellie like a benediction, like a blessing, like the answer to a question she'd been asking her whole life without knowing the words.

And for the first time in longer than she could remember, she didn't feel the urge to argue with it or question it or plan her escape route.

She just felt grateful.

They walked back through the snowy streets of Estrella Ridge—Caleb on one side, Noah on the other, Tripod trotting ahead with his crooked gait, Ellie's ridiculous wings catching on doorframes and making children giggle. Her halo had fallen off completely somewhere back at the square but she didn't care.

She was engaged. She was staying. She was home.

Behind them, the Christmas tree blazed against the night sky, its star steady and bright and refusing to fall. Lights glowed in every window they passed. Smoke curled from chimneys. Somewhere someone was playing Christmas music too loud and singing along even louder.

It was perfect. It was ridiculous. It was everything she'd been afraid to hope for.

And under the wide Colorado sky, with a little boy's mittened hand in hers and the man she loved walking beside her, Ellie Freeman finally—finally—stopped running.

She'd found what she'd been searching for all along, in the last place she'd ever expected to find it.

Home wasn't a place you went back to. Home was what happened when you were brave enough to stop running and let yourself be found.

Epilogue

The June morning was bright and soft, sunlight spilling across the hospital room in a way that made everything feel gentler than it had any right to after twelve hours of labor that had tested every ounce of Ellie's strength and patience.

The cry split the air—loud, indignant, absolutely perfect.

"It's a girl," Doc Martinez announced with the kind of quiet satisfaction that came from delivering babies for thirty years and never getting tired of the miracle. She placed the tiny, squirming bundle on Ellie's chest with practiced gentleness.

Ellie's whole world narrowed to ten tiny fingers and ten tiny toes and a face scrunched up in newborn fury. Warmth and weight and love that hit her like a physical force, stealing her breath and making everything else—the exhaustion, the pain, the fear she'd carried for nine months—dissolve into nothing.

"Oh," she breathed, and couldn't find any other words. Her hands came up to cradle the baby, supporting the impossibly fragile head, feeling the rapid flutter of a heartbeat against her own. "Oh, you're here. You're really here."

Caleb made a sound beside her that was half laugh, half sob. Tears ran down his face freely, unashamedly, like he'd finally stopped pretending that gratitude and joy were things you could keep contained. He reached out with one finger to touch the baby's tiny hand, and she gripped it immediately with the fierce determination of someone who'd already decided she belonged here.

"She's perfect," he whispered, his voice breaking. "Ellie... she's absolutely perfect."

"She is," Ellie agreed, unable to look away from the tiny face that was already changing, relaxing, settling into the world. "She really is."

From the hallway came the unmistakable sound of muffled yelling—Noah being told in increasingly firm tones to use his indoor voice and demonstrating a complete inability to comply with that instruction.

"IS IT A BOY OR A GIRL? CAN I COME IN NOW? I HAVE BEEN WAITING FOREVER AND EVER AND ALSO I BROUGHT FLOWERS BUT TRIPOD TRIED TO EAT THEM!"

Caleb laughed through his tears, the sound watery but genuine. He walked to the door and opened it carefully. "Come in, buddy. Quiet voice, remember?"

The door burst open and Noah skidded in, still in his pajamas—apparently the excitement of baby sister arriving at three a.m. had precluded any thought of actual clothes. Mabel followed behind him, looking surprisingly awake for the early hour, carrying a somewhat mangled bouquet that did indeed appear to have been partially sampled by a three-legged dog.

Noah stopped short at the sight of Ellie holding the baby, his eyes going huge and round. All the noise and energy that usually radiated from him like heat from the sun suddenly went quiet. He tiptoed closer like the room had turned sacred.

"That's her?" he whispered, his voice small and awed. "That's my baby sister?"

"That's her," Ellie said softly, adjusting the blanket so he could see the baby's face more clearly.

Noah stared, mouth slightly open, like he was witnessing something he'd imagined but never quite believed would be real. "She's... really small."

"She's brand new," Caleb said, resting a hand on Noah's shoulder. "She'll get bigger."

"Can I hold her?" The question came out tentative, like Noah was afraid the answer might break something important.

Ellie looked at Caleb, who nodded. They'd talked about this —about how important it was for Noah to feel included, to know that this baby wasn't taking anything away from him but adding to their family.

"Sit in the chair," Ellie said gently. "We'll put her right in your arms."

Noah climbed into the hospital room's oversized recliner with exaggerated care, like he was being sworn into something momentous. He settled himself just so, arranging his arms the way they'd practiced with the doll at home. Caleb lifted the baby carefully and placed her in Noah's waiting arms, keeping his hands close and hovering, ready to catch if needed.

Noah looked down at his sister with an expression of pure wonder. His whole face transformed—the usual mischief and energy replaced by something softer, something that made Ellie's chest ache.

"Hi," he whispered to the baby, his voice barely audible. "I'm your big brother Noah. I'm gonna teach you important stuff. Like how to make really good pancakes, and how to tell when Tripod is lying about not stealing food, and where all the best hiding spots are. And I'm gonna make sure nobody's ever mean to you, okay? That's my job now."

Ellie felt tears slide down her cheeks, the happy kind that came from watching something precious unfold. Caleb moved to stand beside her, his hand finding hers, threading their fingers together.

The baby made a small sound—not quite a cry, more like a squeaky observation about her new circumstances—and Noah's face split into the widest grin Ellie had ever seen.

"She made a noise! Did you hear that? She made a noise AT me! That means she likes me!"

"She definitely likes you," Caleb confirmed, his voice thick with emotion.

Mabel, who'd been standing quietly by the door giving them this moment, finally stepped forward. Her eyes were suspiciously bright behind her glasses, and she was dabbing at them with a tissue.

"She's beautiful," Mabel said, bending to look at the baby. "Absolutely beautiful. What's her name?"

Ellie and Caleb exchanged a glance. They'd talked about this too, late at night when Ellie couldn't sleep because the baby was using her ribcage as a jungle gym. They'd made lists and crossed off names and argued gently about which ones felt right.

"Ruth," Ellie said, her voice catching on the name. "Ruth Sarah Brennan."

Mabel's hand flew to her mouth, her eyes filling with fresh tears. "Oh, honey."

"Ruth for my grandmother," Ellie explained, looking down at the tiny face that was already so loved. "Because she's the reason I came home. And Sarah—" she looked at Caleb, whose jaw was working as he tried to keep his composure "—because this family wouldn't exist without her. Because Noah deserves to have his mom's name carried forward. Because love doesn't end just because someone's gone."

Caleb had to turn away for a moment, his shoulders shaking. When he turned back, his face was wet but his smile was radiant.

"Ruth Sarah," he repeated, testing the sound of it. "Ruthie for short, maybe?"

"Ruthie," Noah said decisively from his chair, looking down at his sister with fierce protectiveness. "That's perfect. Hi, Ruthie. I'm gonna call you Ruthie except when you're in trouble and then I'll use your full name like Daddy does with me."

"That seems fair," Ellie said, laughing through her tears.

They stayed like that for a long moment—Noah holding his baby sister, Caleb standing beside Ellie's bed with their hands clasped, Mabel sniffling quietly by the door. The June sun climbed higher in the sky, painting the hospital room in shades of gold and amber.

Finally, Doc Martinez came back in to check vitals and shoo everyone out so Ellie could rest. Noah reluctantly surrendered the baby back to Ellie's arms, but not before placing a careful kiss on Ruthie's forehead.

"I'll be back soon," he promised the baby seriously. "And I'll bring you something cool from the gift shop. Something way better than flowers."

As Mabel herded Noah out—Noah still talking a mile a minute about all the things he was going to teach his sister—

Caleb settled into the chair beside Ellie's bed.

"How are you feeling?" he asked quietly.

"Exhausted. Sore. Terrified." Ellie looked down at Ruthie, who had fallen asleep, her tiny face peaceful. "And happier than I've ever been in my entire life."

Caleb reached out and ran one finger gently over Ruthie's downy head. "You did amazing. You are amazing."

"We're really doing this," Ellie said, her voice full of wonder. "We're really a family."

"We've been a family for a while now," Caleb reminded her. "The paperwork just made it official."

The wedding had been in March—a small ceremony in the church with the town packed into every pew, Noah as the ring bearer with Tripod as his "assistant," wearing the promised bow tie and Mabel crying so hard she had to be given extra tissues. Pastor Mike had officiated with his gentle humor, and Ellie had worn Ruth's dress from the attic, altered to fit over her growing belly.

She'd stood at the altar in front of everyone who mattered and promised forever to the man who'd pulled her out of a snowbank and offered her something better than rescue: he'd offered her home.

"I still can't believe this is my life," Ellie murmured, adjusting Ruthie's blanket. "A year ago I was running. I was broken. I was convinced I'd lost my chance at any of this."

"Good thing you're stubborn," Caleb said with a soft smile. "And good thing your car went into that particular ditch at that particular time."

"Best accident I ever had."

"Second best," he corrected, nodding at the baby sleeping peacefully in her arms. "She might be the best."

Ellie laughed quietly, careful not to wake Ruthie. "Fair point."

Outside the hospital window, Estrella Ridge was waking up. The mountains stood eternal in the distance, still capped with snow even in June. Church bells rang for morning services. Somewhere someone was mowing their lawn. Life continued in all its ordinary, beautiful ways.

Caleb leaned forward and kissed Ellie's forehead, then Ruthie's.

"Welcome home, little one," he whispered to the baby. "You're going to love it here. Your big brother's going to spoil you rotten, your mom's going to make sure you know you're loved every single day, and this town is going to adopt you so completely you'll never want to leave."

"Just like they did with me," Ellie said softly.

"Just like they did with you."

And sitting there in that hospital room with morning light streaming through the windows, holding her newborn daughter while the man she loved sat beside her and the family they'd built together waited just outside, Ellie Brennan finally understood something she'd spent years searching for.

Home wasn't something you went back to. Home was something you built, brick by brick, choice by choice, day by day. Home was letting yourself be loved by people who'd decided you were worth loving, and then choosing—every single day—to love them back.

She'd spent so long running from the wrong things that she'd almost missed running toward the right thing. But she hadn't missed it. She'd crashed into it, literally and metaphorically, and it had caught her. Estrella Ridge had caught her. Caleb had caught her. This family had caught her. And she was never, ever letting go.

Caleb's quiet laughter was the last thing she heard before exhaustion pulled her under into dreams of summer days and baby giggles and a future that stretched out before her like a gift she finally believed she deserved to unwrap.

www.ingramcontent.com/pod-product-compliance
Lightning Source LLC
Chambersburg PA
CBHW051701180726
48283CB00004B/1166